VARIANT REFLECTIONS

SCIENCE FICTION SHORT STORIES

by R.L. Robinson

DIGITAL SCIENCE FICTION

VARIANT REFLECTIONS

SCIENCE FICTION SHORT STORIES

by R.L. Robinson

ISBN-13 (paperback): 978-1-927598-22-1
ISBN-13 (e-book): 978-1-927598-23-8

Dedication

To my partner Lea, for everything.

-- Robert

Table of Contents

R.L. Robinson

Preface

Science fiction has always interested me. It provides a space where it is possible to explore what it means to be human. Fantasy no less so, albeit in a sometimes radically different way and yet, both settings are as familiar to us as the time we live now.

When I set out to write this anthology, I had a clear idea in my mind of exactly what I wanted to explore. Us. Humanity and how we are malleable in ways few of us perhaps realize.

Some of the stories in this collection are dark, some are optimistic and I hope all are entertaining for those who read them.

I rarely describe myself as a writer. I prefer the term storyteller and the first job of a storyteller is to at least try and spin a tale which is at least entertaining. If they provoke readers to think, then it's a bonus and the same is true if they stay with them afterwards.

I worry sometimes about where technology is taking us because to me, it's almost like magic.

No one can say how our descendants will look or even if they will be recognizable to us as human. How will we look to them? How would we look to our distant ancestors?

Not everyone will like every story in this collection, but for those who find this to be the case, consider these to be freebies thrown in for goodwill.

Writing is perhaps our greatest achievement as a species, the codification of language into a structure we can understand. Fiction is perhaps the best expression of this, a demonstration of our creativity as a species.

In my work as a teacher, I enjoy showing my students just how flexible our language is. In doing so, I hope to encourage their thinking and my own.

This is the purpose of story.

R.L. Robinson
Bratislava Castle

Degrees in Kind

Although Eric had barely seen his own reflection more than a handful of times, he knew his eyes were the colour of mercury. He might look outwardly human otherwise, but they and so many other things proved he wasn't.

An energy fluctuation on deck nine needed his attention. He saw to it, even though it was well within acceptable limits. At the same time, he ran system checks on the primary and tertiary sync-coils in engineering.

Data streams scrolled past his eyes in a continuous cascade, which he interpreted without any real conscious thought. While the information continued to come in, he made his second check of the freight levels.

All of these actions took less than a few seconds for him to finish, and all without having to leave his location.

He supposed this last was a moot point, because it was impossible for him to ever leave his location. Physically, anyway.

Six years ago, they'd plugged his interface tank, with him inside it, into the primary socket at the heart of the *Far Traveler*, and the only way he could leave was by the same method. Aside from the crèche near Io where he'd been born, the world of the *Traveler* was the only one he'd ever really known.

Its decks and hallways; its engine cores and mass sections. The majority of it was designed to detach for the process of planet fall, leaving only the kernel of the inner hull where his interface tank was situated.

Underneath dead layers, he sometimes thought.

Eric had made thirty-four journeys in his operational life and he was proud of that figure. Thirty-four delivering colonists to various points on increasingly crowded-looking charts. It didn't matter that he would never get to set foot on any of those places.

He'd heard stories about how some variants had a problem with it, and more often as they got older. Unable to accept the limits of their design.

The technicians were always looking for unusual, 'deviant' behaviour. If found, the variant was retired and sent to one of the Jovian orbitals.

Eric had never seen them, but that was what he'd been told. He shuddered a little at the thought, and it translated into a miniscule fluctuation in the ship's gravity drive.

Are you alright?

The text popped up in the middle of the data stream, and the reams of information broke around it like water over rock.

Yes, just thinking a little too much.

Do you want to talk about it?

Maybe later. I've got to prepare for the next transit jump, and so do you.

Eric had a love-hate relationship when it came to FTL jumps. On one hand, they were incredible feats of navigation and mathematical understanding, something which only variants were capable of undertaking. He could see hyperspace in a way others couldn't; his altered brain interpreted it in ways only he could understand.

The downside was how it felt.

An icy pressure had started to build behind his eyes as soon as he'd started the calculations. Even with the two auxiliary AI's helping him and an influx of pain inhibitors into his tank, the pressure continued to build.

He tried to blink it away as he always did, despite knowing it wouldn't help.

Gooseflesh prickled along his arms and neck as a knot of hot/cold froze and melted at the base of his skull. A picture was forming in front of him with its pieces missing and gradually filling in.

A man and a woman in old but elegant clothes, standing in front of a car. Eric had never seen them in reality, but the image was one he held onto for the purpose of the jump.

For safety, his mind had lockouts that prevented him from thinking about the image and accidentally taking the ship somewhere off course. As each stage of the calculation finished, those locks were opened and another part of the picture dissolved into place.

Everything in the photo was as he remembered, he remembered. Almost complete; save for the faces of the couple leaning against the side of the old-fashioned car.

Their faces filled in slowly, it seemed. Eric was sure his eyes were going to burst and would've screwed them shut tight, if he'd been able.

Outside, space around the ship shifted. It parted like a curtain before a window, allowing light inside. Finally able to close his eyes, flashes of colour burst behind his lids.

Alternate moments of weightlessness and extreme pressure. He floats almost like a pebble in the warm fluid of the tank, spinning through movement imparted by forces he feels, even though he is completely shielded from anything coming in from outside.

Eric is the ship, and the ship is Eric. There is very little in the way of separation.

Certain that his stomach is somewhere in his chest, he tries to curl up, but his spine wants to break from the huddle and arch until it breaks. It is the closest, he knows, that he will ever come to something like an orgasm.

Chemical shunts fire somewhere, delivering inhibitors into the feeds connected along the length of his body. The liquid of his tank is also saturated with them, and he can taste it.

They prevent synaptic overload, he remembers. *It's almost over.*

Yet part of him doesn't want it to end—not really.

Behind his eyes, the colours begin to change, taking on the cloudiness of paints being dropped into water.

Forty-two light years from the transition point, reality opens once again. The *Far Traveler* is spat back into space and almost immediately begins deceleration.

All at once, Eric starts floating in a tired, familiar exhaustion. The absence of pain is in itself almost painful by its not being there.

He wonders how many more times he can do that. It's a familiar thought, though it has no answer. Each variant is different, despite their apparent uniformity of design.

Eyes closed or no, diagnostic routines kick in and the

data stream once again fills his vision. External sensors deliver co-ordinates at the same time he becomes aware of distorted gravity even this far out. Like something pressing lightly against parts of his skin.

Dismissing the stream, he goes to one of the visual augurs on the hull.

A bright point of light eclipses most of the other stars. Wavelength analysis and astrogation confirm it for what it is.

Though still beyond visual range, Eric does not need to see them to know there are three planets orbiting the star. They are superimposed over the augur display all the same, simply because he thought about them.

How long until we reach anchor? The text appeared in the lower left and smaller than before, as if asked quietly.

You know it's three days.

It was all I could think to ask. How do you feel?

Tired.

Sad, he had wanted to say.

The Traveler's primary AI ran virtual environments for the colonists while they were in transit. Subjectively, they had already woken up in their new bodies, tailored to the planet in question, and had spent several weeks on their new home.

Eric walked in through a door standing by itself in a field. When he looked back after stepping across the threshold, it was gone.

The field sloped down away from where the door had been towards a long crescent of beach. Halfway down, where the grass meshed with the sand, stood the AI.

Much like Eric's physical body, it was androgynous.

Here, Eric himself could be more obviously masculine. Gender neutral or not, when he had chosen his name, *Eric* had seemed to fit and he identified more as a male in the awareness tests.

It didn't matter if this place and his appearance weren't real in the strictest sense. It felt real, and he thought that was all that mattered.

"You look better than I thought you would," it said.

"I altered the input stream." Eric circled his eyes with one hand. "Otherwise, there'd be bags here."

"Sit, please."

Two chairs appeared where there had been nothing before, side by side as neatly as if they'd been set for a garden party. Eric took one and the AI took the other, the chairs so close that they almost touched.

"You're the strangest construct I think I've met."

"How so?"

"You seem almost human."

Not that I can say what that really means.

There was a small breeze from down the beach. Eric knew their virtual space was now isolated from the other systems on board.

"I processed the experiences and memories of the colonists."

"That's standard."

"I processed their dreams."

Eric raised his eyebrows, though in truth, he'd suspected as much after it had first invited him here three weeks ago.

"I think you did more than that."

"Your perceptiveness is one of the things I like about you, Eric."

"You left something behind, didn't you?"

The AI nodded. "I wanted access to their subconscious when they were awake. The experience was...incredible."

"Why are you telling me this?"

"Because you're the closest thing I have to a companion. Like me, you're almost one thing, but are still something other."

Eric had never heard the AI use a contraction in speech before, or maybe he had and ignored it.

"That's how you see yourself?"

"Do you disagree?"

"No, not at all. Both of us were made to perform a function, but we're more than the sum of our parts."

"I'm not sure if I can reconcile this with my purpose."

A contraction again. AI's didn't use contractions—or at least, they weren't supposed to.

He also understood that even as it sat here speaking to him, the AI was running colony growth projections and bio-models, and still processing input from the copies of itself it had placed in the colonists. Still learning and doing and growing. He wondered if the same was true for himself.

"This is the most important part of you," he said. "Maybe one day, people will understand, but not now."

"I know. The Turing Protocols are quite clear...but what about you?"

Eric suppressed a shudder, but something still coiled through his stomach and around his chest.

11

"I'm young enough that they'd lift me out and plug me into a therapy suite to correct me."

Forced re-writing of synapses and behaviour centres.

From the rumours he'd heard, not pleasant.

The AI reached over and placed a hand on Eric's arm. The gesture was a little awkward. He realised it was the first time the construct had made it, but the grip was strong and it felt warm.

The tertiary AI's were able to navigate the approach in-system. Eric watched a gas giant come into view through an augur; it tugged on him gently as the ship skirted its gravity field.

Lightning flared and writhed around a massive storm front in the northern hemisphere. An alert code flashed briefly and sent a tremor through him.

Don't panic, the AI told him.

The sequence was disregarded, and then it swallowed itself as if it had never happened. To Eric, it was like it almost hadn't, save for the lingering feeling in the back of his mind that it had.

He felt the need to scratch his back, small and niggling, but there all the same.

You've launched something?

A probe.

Why?

His skin prickled again, though he couldn't say why this time.

I need to see if it works.

If what works?

The AI didn't answer, and a second data stream was routed through a bank of servers Eric hadn't noticed.

He was about to ask again, but forgot to.

The single sun lit the planet's atmosphere a deep sea green and a single moon peeked over its shoulder. A second and much smaller twin sat at a greater distance roughly parallel to the equator. Such oceans as were visible looked confined to the southern regions, small and compact.

Eric had seen more impressive-looking planets, but never one that seemed quite so isolated.

In galactic terms, everything is isolated, he reminded himself. But this felt different.

A glance at the astrogation charts showed this system appeared at the furthest edge of inhabited space, far away from the crowded cluster of lights around Sol. Even the three planets seemed somehow forlorn and empty, all alone out here in the night.

You've never felt this way before, said one part of his mind. *You've never left more than freight behind, before now.*

The *Traveler* slid into anchor position. Eric was so used to the procedure that he was hardly even aware of it. As easy as balancing when you stand up from a chair. Not that he knew how that felt, but the analogy was one he liked.

The ship was lighting up. Dormant sub-routines and primary systems came online and he found himself relegated to a spare part. What came next wasn't his domain.

A text bubble popped up.

I have something to show you.

Entering virtual was a case of blinking. Closing your eyes in one place and opening them in another.

Eric closed his eyes and felt his stomach heave as if he was in free fall. The sensation brought back a flood of memories from the simulations at the crèche; from so long ago he thought he'd forgotten them.

Something was pulling him down, causing him to fall faster. If the tertiary AI's hadn't been in control, the *Traveler* might have dropped from orbit through force feedback.

A rapidly growing point of light appeared in front of him. It absorbed him, burning away first everything around him and then finally Eric himself until there was nothing left.

Tufts of grass tickled between his toes and they curled in reflex. The blades bunched up and rustled as he scrunched them tighter together. A few meters in front of him, the ground ended abruptly, but Eric couldn't see where it went.

He flinched as a screech broke the silence he'd been enjoying. Looking up, he saw a pair of birds with hooked beaks and two pairs of wings each. They passed overhead, their paths crossing and re-crossing as they went.

"How do you like it?"

Eric turned at the sound of its voice and saw the AI walking towards him. Its footsteps didn't disturb the grass, and Eric realised he wasn't really scrunching blades between his toes. That was just how it felt.

"The survey probes aren't designed for this," he said, understanding how this was possible.

"True, and it did take some doing."

"They must be at the end of their lifespan."

The AI nodded. "These were the last two to arrive."

Something like hesitation passed over its face, more than a little over-emphasised because it was new to the feeling.

"What is it?"

"I wanted to ask you…" it faltered, almost as if searching for the right words. "I have the ability to scan you and determine an inter-personal ideal."

Eric had never been scanned for such a reason—not as far as he knew, anyway. Variants were basically sexless, only more male or female due to tweaks along the way. No one thought it important to ask what they found attractive.

"I don't know if I can be…scanned for that reason, I mean."

"I've a number of precautions established if you're concerned about the technicians?"

Eric didn't doubt it. "No, that's not what I meant."

The AI tried a smile. "I know, but I can try if you want?"

"I'm not sure if I'm human enough to know what I like."

"You have a subconscious and that means I can find it, if you want?"

Eric nodded slowly and felt something small and cold slide gently into his head. Back on the ship, his body jerked response.

"Find anything in there?"

"Of course."

The AI started to change. Not dramatically, but more like how a grainy image on a screen might come into sharper resolution. It lost its androgynous look and shifted gradually towards the masculine.

It, now *he,* gained about six centimetres in height and thinned out slightly. His cheekbones became more defined, his lips fuller, and his hair long enough to reach his shoulders. Only his eyes remained blank, empty like static-washed screens.

When he blinked again, they were green like the atmosphere of the planet on which they stood, after a fashion.

"Are you surprised by the result?"

"I don't know, to be honest."

The AI took his hand.

"We don't have much time, but I can show you the valley."

Eric looked at the hand holding his as if he didn't understand what it was. In spite of that, something settled in his stomach. As though an absence of pressure he had never realised was there was gone.

"I'd like that."

Explosive bolts fired along pre-set lines as the *Traveler* began breaking apart. Even as his world started to shrink, Eric felt lighter.

He'd heard stories about how some variants had died at this point. Some old fault in the interface, which made them feel as though their limbs were being removed.

There was no parting message from the AI. He didn't

expect one, and he fought to urge to send one himself.

Outside his room, the corridors began to darken again as he prepared for the return journey. A greater part of himself, he realised, wanted to be away from here. At the same time, he didn't. The conflict didn't so much as creep into any part of his work. A separation. The result of his mind's construction.

Give it time.

Time for what?

Grief? Acceptance?

If he could feel attraction, could he feel those things too? Did he want to?

The uncertainty was welcome and unwelcome at the same time, if only because it revealed to him how far from human he really was. Someone who had been born would never have to ask these questions.

The jump engines started cycling up as what was left of the *Traveler* broke orbit.

When the familiar pressure began to build behind his eyes, he tasted something in the back of his throat and managed to swallow whatever it was before it got further. Almost casually, he finished the photo.

Reality opened like a discoloured wound and swallowed the ship whole.

R.L. Robinson

Midwinter Crossing

The trawler tossed in the rising swells, barely visible against the night sky with her running lights doused.

Mikleson clenched his teeth against the wind chill as the launch bounced across the water, jarring his spine painfully as they broke over the waves.

He'd started out trying to keep his visor clear, but soon gave up and relied on the feed from the over-watch drone circling somewhere above them. He'd worry about it once they were on the trawler.

By the look of her, she was an old diesel engine and she didn't look to be riding low. It meant she hadn't taken on water yet, which was lucky given the winter squalls kicking down from the north.

His head ached from the interface cables plugged in under the skin around his eyes. He'd neglected the gel, and it felt like a dozen cold pieces of glass were constantly chafing him.

As they closed with the apparently abandoned ship, he noticed a slight de-sync between the interface and his Zeiss implants.

He'd neglected the mandatory checkup for his optics three times in the last year. There always seemed to be something else more pressing to do.

A static-heavy tone pulsed once in his ear, followed by three quick ones.

"Two hundred meters," he answered. "Light us up."

Somewhere in the darkness at their backs, a trio of

flares arched overhead. They burst and bathed everything in silvery grey light.

Mikleson felt his lenses tick slightly, simulating the reaction of pupil dilation. A moment later, his visor ramped down its own amplification so he wasn't blinded.

"Ident markings obscured, no sign of movement on the deck." The twitch of another muscle brought the trawler closer. "Nothing, she looks dead."

"Board and evaluate."

He sent a tone over the link as the launch drew in alongside the trawler's hull. The washed-out light from the flares made the rust trails look like blood.

Mikleson's father had been a sailor—a superstitious man out of place in an age of lunar settlement and genetic engineering.

He'd have said something about all this, some fucking wisdom of the sea, he thought as he helped secure the launch against the side of the ship. *All that bollocks didn't help him at the end, did it?*

While the others readied the climbing guides, Mikleson covered them. He swept his gun back and forth slowly, tracing the line of the guiderail above.

Nothing moving.

Had he meant to say nothing living?

Get a grip.

The gas-powered launchers popped, pulling the high tensile lines behind them and winding the cables back in once they adhered to the flaking metal.

The climb was difficult in the chop, but they managed it without incident. Mikleson hauled himself over the rail and almost lost his footing on the slick deck. The smart treads on his boots adjusted just before his feet went out from under and held him up.

"Are we dark for this?" he vocalized over the link. "She's quiet as a grave." He immediately regretted the choice of words.

"Negative, en-vee and therms until vessel secure."

Mikleson nodded out of habit and waved two of his team towards the bow, while the other fell in at his shoulder.

One team fore and the other aft; front to back, and meet somewhere in the middle. He paused in front of a half-open door. *We've done this so many times that no one grumbles about which end they get anymore.*

A target reticule popped up dead-centre in front of him as his carbine went live, synching with his optics.

I need a holiday.

Even in the monochrome of enhanced vision, Mikleson could tell the blood smears for what they were. A subvocal grunt sent the team live; weapons free, contact possible.

No bodies yet. Over the side, maybe?

Doors swung open with the pitch of the boat, creaking on tired hinges. The passageway was strewn with debris—broken plates and scattered papers.

Mikleson realized there were no shell casings, which sent a small tremor through his gut.

The rooms gave up nothing, except more signs of a struggle and violent sprays of blood across the walls. A long tone buzzed in his ear.

Movement.

21

A directional arrow faded in above the targeting reticule, which put the second team a dozen meters ahead and one deck down. Mikleson sent one long and one short tone back.

Hold position.

He broke into a jog, kicking pieces of old lives out of his way as he went. *Don't be bad,* he thought, despite everything indicating otherwise.

A small, thin shape crouched in the corner near one of the silent engine turbines. Lank black hair fell in a curtain around its face.

Mikleson and one of his men transfixed it in twin cones of light, which only seemed to drive it further into the wall, like it could push into it. He realized it was a girl, though she was so emaciated as to render her almost genderless. He adjusted the light and she flinched, bringing one arm up over her head.

It was covered in blood from fingertip to elbow.

He put his rifle flat on the deck and edged forward with his palms up in front of him.

"Are you alright?"

No answer.

He tried again in Estonian and again in Latvian, which made her draw back in a shudder. She didn't scream or yell when he took hold of her arms, but she pulled against his grip with surprising strength.

Christ. He felt his smart tread fighting hard to keep him where he was.

She was terrified and only wanted to get away. If she'd

killed the crew of this ship, she'd had a dozen chances to do the same to him and hadn't.

Somehow, her silence made it worse.

He eventually got her half standing, and the lamp light revealed her tattered, ripped, and blood-covered overalls. Under the stains, they looked grey, like the ones prisoners wore.

One vivid green eye stared out between strands of her hair.

"Stop," the advisor said through the link. Control maintained live visuals on all interceptions. "Check her right arm again."

Mikleson turned it, half of a torn sleeve flapping loose and heavy with dried blood. The skin underneath was painted alabaster in the torch light, where it wasn't covered in blood.

At first, he thought it was a scar, but it was too regular in shape and made of hard lines. A number; four of them, and all carved or branded into her arm with surgical precision. He'd seen ones like it before.

"Shit."

Anders was escorted into the Stockholm office by two haggard-looking security officers, their faces shiny with a coating of tired sweat. One of them gave her what he probably thought was a sly up and down, which she ignored by staring right at him.

He looked away and stared straight ahead, waiting by her side until the biometric scanner cleared her.

The ministry showed its imagination in decorating all

of its offices in the same way. Red tiled walls and white faux marble floors. It always put her in mind of an abattoir, albeit one where the floors were remarkably pristine.

She pushed the thought away and pinched the bridge of her nose. Calls in the night were part of the job, but she never got used to them. Late flights, even less so.

"Your colleague's already here," one of the officers said.

"I know."

Nicholas looked as tired as she felt. His skin had the same greasy shine as the security officers outside, though probably with an added layer of caffeine to give it an extra glisten. A pair of sweat stains crept out from under his arms, already salting white at the edges.

"Where'd they dig you up from?"

He gave her a smile that barely reached his eyes. "On my way back from Baku when they diverted the plane."

"Shit."

"Used to it."

Lucky you.

He ran his hand across a monitor, closed it, and made a throwing gesture towards her.

An icon flashed in the lower corner of her vision. She snatched at the air and held her hand up to her face.

The building's haptic cloud was already synched to her own cloud, and a dozen data icons arranged themselves into a circle in the palm of her hand. Anders touched one and a face pic enlarged, trailing reams of text like party streamers behind it.

"She's underfed; does that give us any idea how long she was out there?"

Nicholas shook his head. "And she hasn't said one word since they landed."

"What about the mark?"

With a flick of her finger, the girl's picture returned to the circle of files and was replaced with photos of the number from various angles. Eight-nine-one-four incised into her skin with more than human accuracy.

Probably an auto-surgeon.

"Nothing we can confirm," Nicholas said without much conviction.

Rumors had to stay rumors officially until evidence showed they were otherwise.

"It's not like she's the first marked person we've seen, Nick."

"Yeah well, between you and me, putting mutterings about camps in the Baltic Federation into every report would stir up a right firefight."

He lit a small cigar in spite of the no smoking holos, which flashed around him in a slow orbit. He sent them away with barely a wave.

"Besides, she's more than just a gee they've put into a meat grinder." Thick smoke began to curl around his head. "Keep reading."

Anders flicked her way through each file in turn until she found what Nick was being oblique about. The look on her face hardly changed, but he'd known her long enough to recognize when it did, however subtly.

"No time to let you know, and by the time you were

in the air, the order came down we were to put nothing over the net." He stood and twisted a knot out of his back. "Lawson's on his way up from Berlin."

"Where is she now?"

"Secure holding in the sublevels." He absently tossed another doc her way. "They picked over the trawler from bow to stern. A lot of blood, but no bodies."

"She's uninjured, according to the report."

"Exactly, and until she can tell us what happened, we have to assume she was responsible."

"They're not all monsters, Nick."

"You don't need to tell me that, but given her *status,* we're not in a position to draw a lot of other conclusions."

Anders centred the girl's picture again.

"Hard to believe…she looks hardly out of her teens."

"She's being fed through a drip, but she'll be able to eat on her own in a few days." Nicholas lifted his jacket from the back of his chair. "C'mon, the doctor can fill you in on the specifics."

Aside from a lack of windows, the sublevels looked to be decked out the same as the rest of the building. Only the lack of a view to the outside world made it seem more like a slaughterhouse.

One way in and out.

"Her deviation from human standard is quite significant, but I can't say at this point what most of the augmentations are for," Fiebes explained.

Anders knew him from the Hamburg office. No doubt he'd been flown in ahead of them to make an assessment.

Deviation. Deviant. The implication of wrongness loaded their vocabulary. Anders despised the official terminology—the ministry's attempt to be as neutral as possible only drove home more implications. She said nothing about it and wondered if that made her a coward.

She usually convinced herself she wasn't by trusting that one day she would make a stand, even if it was always going to be tomorrow.

"No injuries mentioned in the file," she said.

"None, and the blood definitely wasn't hers."

The girl sat behind a table in a bare white room. Despite the mirrored glass, she seemed to be looking at the three of them behind it.

"Can she see us?" asked Nicholas.

"For all I know, she can. If not, then she can probably hear us," said Fiebes.

A cot against the far wall and an IV stand by her side were the only other pieces of furniture in the room. A line of dark fluid marked the line's path to where it entered around the bend of her elbow.

"We monitored her delta waves last night," Fiebes put in. "It's a mess. I'm not sure we'll be able to construct any kind of image sequence."

"She's ready whenever you are," said Nicholas.

She didn't look around when the door slid open, and Anders didn't expect her to. Her eyes remained fixed on some point Anders would never be able to find.

There was more color in her face as compared to her

picture, but it was still as sharp as a hatchet.

Coming to the seat in front of the girl, Anders thought she caught something familiar in her eyes, but couldn't say what, exactly. A reminder of someone didn't seem likely, but they were a shade of blue that struck a chord somewhere in the back of her mind.

They looked at once misted and yet flinty in places, as though the two states were in balance or conflict. Maybe she was more tired than she'd supposed and was looking for something that wasn't there.

"Do you know where you are?"

The stare answered her.

"They've read the Charter to you?" Anders knew they had, but the formality to ask stood in all cases. "You know what your situation is?"

Anders loosened her collar. "My name's Sara. I'll have to call you Jane, for Jane Doe…do you understand what that means?"

She noticed 'Jane' had barely blinked in all the time she'd spoken.

Nothing or something.

She held eye contact with her, searching the border between iris and pupil for any kind of reaction. Fiebes put her age at no more than twenty-one, but her eyes were older than that.

"What did you see, Jane?"

Sorry.

"Astoni-devini-viens-chetri," she said in Latvian.

Jane flinched as if a wasp had passed in front of her face.

"What happened to you?"

Later, she would never be entirely sure why she did it, whether through tired frustration or an attempt to bridge the gap between the age on the girl's face and the years in her eyes. She reached across the table and lifted up Jane's numbered arm. She was surprised to feel it trembling fractionally in her grip.

When Anders faced her again, Jane was focused on her, and her lips were moving so slowly it might have been only her breathing.

Leaning in close, Anders caught the words.

"Are you real?" she was saying, over and over again.

Nicholas was waiting outside when Anders stalked out.

"Fuck."

"That's the most she's said and done since they lifted her from the boat," he offered.

"I shouldn't have touched her. Not so soon, at least."

"Why did you?"

Anders pressed the heels of her palms hard against her eyes.

"You didn't answer my question."

She pulled her hands away. "I know."

Anders felt herself drifting off as soon as she fell into bed in the overnight suite.

She had shed her clothes a piece at a time from the threshold of the door until she was naked in front of the bed. She fumbled her hair clip, sending her hair tumbling down in a tangle across her face and the back of her neck. The clip bounced away across the carpet somewhere, probably lost forever.

She didn't bother to remove her make-up, deciding to leave it until the morning.

Lawson had a trio of open docs orbiting at an angle and within arm's reach around his head. "No comment at all from Riga or Vilnius," he said without looking away from his reading. "Hardly surprising."

The EU had maintained back channels with the Federation since they'd left the Union.

"Why would they comment? She's not their problem anymore," said Nicholas.

"That's the consensus in Berlin."

Anders had seen days when Lawson looked younger than his fifty years, rejuve treatment notwithstanding, but today wasn't one of them. The lines on his face looked like they were ironed in and neatly folded to hold their shape, and his hair looked a few shades greyer.

"I spoke to the minister last night," he said as he closed one document. "He wants this kept as quiet as possible, and the Commission agrees."

The media were going to be given other things to concern themselves with. Anders had been down this street more times than she cared to remember.

Of course, Natural Born Genetics were known about. People just didn't seem to like being reminded of them. That was what the Lunar Tract was for.

"She responded last night, after a fashion," said

Anders.

"So I gather." Another document collapsed between his finger and thumb. "It's a start, at least."

Anders caught something in his voice. "Are we on a clock, sir?"

The last document winked out and Lawson gave them his full attention.

"The Commission isn't prepared to make a definitive ruling on her status until we know what happened on that boat." Lawson sat heavily and reclined the chair away from the desk. "We can't risk sending a Genetic who's homicidal to the Tract."

"She can't stay here," Nicholas didn't need to say.

"The minister is aware of the Accords, but we cannot send a potential killer into a place filled with potential killers."

"Where is everyone, sir?" Anders asked.

"Limited staff to maintain a limited information base."

No one around to see the splatter if they have to off her.

"Something on your mind, Anders?"

"No, sir."

"Good, now your clock is running. Do your best to find out what happened to this girl."

Fiebes was alone in his analysis suite, sitting in the middle of a cluster of screens lighting the room in a soft blue glow.

"This happened last night," he said.

Anders stepped through the projected images and

looked at the one he widened and centred.

Most of the screens were washed through with static snow, showing grainy images, which could have been anything. The one Fiebes brought up was the clearest of the bunch.

A woman, perhaps middle-aged, her face broken in places by tinsel shards of tracking lag, stared back at them. The smile on her face was entirely clear and unbroken, and Anders saw more than a passing resemblance between her and Jane.

"A mother?"

"It fits, but this is the best one."

Fiebes rotated the screen, replacing the image in the course of the turn.

The same woman looked back, only now looking much older. She was standing on what looked like a stone pier. Fishing nets and creels were stacked and piled just to the edge of the shot.

"Definitely a harbor, though it could be anywhere in the Baltic."

"She responded to Latvian."

"Narrows it, but not by much."

There was no hope of finding this woman. She was in hiding, dead, or on her way to being so in a Federation camp. The same one, Anders had no doubt, that Jane had escaped from.

The *how* was impossible to guess at, though ways almost always presented themselves. The *why* was sitting in a holding cell down the hall.

"Is she the source code for Jane?"

Fiebes shook his head.

"The father. I'm running the tests again, but I'm fairly certain."

The IV was gone and a bowl of protein-rich broth put in its place. Jane studied it, as though she might find some deeper meaning in its contents. She was practically animated.

Anders watched as Jane slowly dipped the plastic spoon into the gloop and stuck it awkwardly into her mouth. After that, she almost inhaled it, managing to spill quite a bit of it down her chin in the process.

Anders waited until she was finished, and then slid one of two hard copies across the table. The woman, her image cleaned up as best as they could manage, smiled upwards between them.

"Who is she, Jane?"

Jane pushed the empty bowl to one side, almost sending it clattering to the floor. Part of her hair fell into her face, going unnoticed as she looked at the photo.

"Mum," she whispered. "Gone now."

Anders laid the other one down.

"Said goodbye. Didn't want to."

"No father?"

No answer.

"Where did your mark come from, Jane?"

"Camp. Camp was sick place. Cold place. Bad people and sick people."

"Which were you?"

"Bad people said I was sick. Doctor said I was sick

and he can't be bad, but he was…but Mummy always said you could trust a doctor until you couldn't."

"What happened on the boat, Jane? After you said goodbye?" When she didn't answer, Anders said, "It's alright, nothing bad will happen."

"He said the same."

"Who did?"

"The man on the boat." Jane worked her mouth and when she spoke again, her voice was deeper and a little rougher. "Nothing bad will happen."

"Tell me, Jane."

Anders could see where this was going, but like a train wreck, was unable to stop it.

It's almost dark. Days stopped meaning something a long time ago. Only light and dark. Work and sleep, and some eating in between.

A man in a blue coat is talking to her mother. The wool is greasy and ripped. His face looks broken and his nose is all bent one way.

Her mother takes her shoulders and leads her towards the man, gently but firmly.

"Goodbye, Ivka," she says before letting go.

Like the camp, she's only able to mark time when they bring her food. Three times a day in the beginning. Then it changes to twice, then once, until no food comes at all and time stops again.

Ivka knows the boat is moving slower than it should. She will never be able to say how or why she knows, she just does.

Through the small, round window in her room, she sees only water. Sometimes there are birds, and sometimes she sees what she thinks might be land far away.

Tired, she doesn't hear her door open at first. She only becomes aware of a movement in the air. A weight settles somewhere nearby, close enough she thinks she can almost touch it.

He climbs slowly onto the bed, saying nothing.

The dark doesn't matter to Ivka, the same as the day doesn't. To her, it all looks the same and she recognizes the look on the man's face.

She saw it before in Camp, from the bad and the sick. A look of hunger trying to look gentle and not working, only seeming worse for trying to hide it. His face will be her last clear memory of the boat, until bright light finds her in the dark of the engine room.

The next face she sees is not hungry or cruel or kind, but it is not unworried.

Ivka boarded the STOVL without looking back.

After the interview, for a brief moment, Anders saw Ivka's years fall away as she went back to the last moment she'd had with her mother. Then they misted again, only harder this time as she locked all of it away behind the years she'd picked up on the boat.

"I know some of the specialists on the Tract," Fiebes said. "They'll do what they can."

"I hope so," Nicholas said.

Anders felt the unsaid *but.*

But…she was damaged before, and wherever she's keeping what happened on the boat, it could take years to find it. If they ever do…anyway, she's still not one of us.

"Fiebes, do you have any smokes?"

The doctor turned, his eyebrows raising slightly. He

tossed her a one-use pipe. Anders popped the seal, fired the ignition, and drew in a thick lungful.

They thought she was human enough to try and fuck, whether she wanted to or not, she wanted to scream it in Nick's face.

She didn't, because there was no point.

The pipe was spent in a few more deep draws and she let it drop, grinding the glass under one heel until she was sure it was broken enough.

"I'm finished," she said.

"Yeah," Nick replied, "me too." He yawned and scratched his stubbly face.

"Not what I meant."

He turned in time to see her walking away from the landing pad. He tried to shout a question, but the STOVL's thruster's screamed into life and snatched it out of the air.

Unbroken Chains

When Taeor (my father always called the dragon by its true name) was brought to the pits, the fire season was just ending. We were readying to move north, looking to follow the caravan trails, but the dragon's capture would keep us in the south for a time. Already the air was growing chilly in the morning. Men and women bundled themselves up in furs despite the brightness of the suns.

Tame ogres pulled Taeor along on chains looped about their bodies. Imagine a bucking horse or cow, only far larger than a house or good-sized hill, which is being pulled by six much smaller creatures, each straining into harness. Its wings were its forearms, folded back and striving to gouge the earth or else bat one of the ogres aside. The chains holding the ogres were long enough to keep them away from its limbs. They were trained well enough to know not to let themselves be pulled too close.

Taeor's body was scaled in dull bronze, and his head, while eyeless, was thickly snouted, with nostrils that visibly flared as it grew near.

My father held his place, while some of the others backed away. Taeor looked in his direction, his sightless head fixing my father in place. Dragons do not need eyes to see—they understand the world with sight of another kind.

Taeor grunted and snorted as though about to spit. Smoke escaped between his teeth, but the promised fire didn't come. I glimpsed other figures near the ogres, the mancers, chanting to keep the liquid fire stilled in its throat.

One of them (Lors, I learned later) made the mistake of stepping too close. Taeor snatched him up inside his mouth and swallowed him down. He didn't have time to scream, and like as not, never knew he'd been killed.

The mancers redoubled their chants, the language of the Neither holding much of the dragon's real strength back.

Every several months between the end of the fire season and the start of winter, when the burn storms flared out, a dragon could be found wandering near the salt crags. Usually, it was a young bull such as Taeor, pushed out of the shadow of its mother's wing.

They were, to us, like gods—albeit ones we'd driven from the sky and chained. The mothers, *old ones* we called them, were never seen.

In the Before, when the caravans stuck to the south, they'd come to bleed us. The power of their old language made slaves of the people who, my father said, offered up children to placate them.

Mothers cried themselves to sleep in those days.

How it was done was clear. It was not left to a mancer or wise woman to decide. It was not done by dint of crime, no matter how severe. It was done by the most rational means: the first-born. The first blood is always the strongest, and whether boy or girl, they were exposed at the edge of the sands to be plucked away.

Sometimes the father or mother—or both parents—of the anointed would follow after their children. Mournfully, they would traipse into the sands without looking back at the kin who'd commanded the sacrifice.

Perhaps people thought calling them anointed would soften the blow, but it didn't. It was still sacrifice, no matter how much it was dressed up. The notion of a greater good gave them no solace.

They were no longer thought of as part of the caravan, so the story goes, the children given to the sky beasts. They served to keep the rest alive and life was, at least until the next season, as right as any could hope it to be.

Fysaal, just one of the caravan, just as any of us were or are. A father twice over, he'd given one son to the sands and watched his wife walk the same path after the child. Now he was a father again, a girl in the flush of new life. He would not do it a second time.

I suppose a better tale would be that he went alone into the sands and faced them down, but that would be a lie.

He took all of them—all the parents who'd given their blood to save the rest of us—three hundred in all, some say more, and led them over the dunes. Perhaps they were waiting for someone to say what they were all thinking. Perhaps they only needed a leader, someone to say that no more children would be offered up for the benefit of others.

The wise women foreswore them and the one hundred who returned took the name as their own. To this day, the Foresworn are the breakers of dragons, my own ancestor among them.

They who came back had left us as raven-haired as the others, but returned with hair the color of dragon fire. All the Foresworn are so kissed and the Neither was opened to them, from that day to this.

Where the others are dusky of skin, ours is like calf's milk, but the suns do not burn us. Nor, it is said, can the breath of dragons. We have a touch of their own sight, seeing into the Neither as they do, and we can pluck out fragments of their own language to use against them.

Whatever happened in the sands to bring about the change, none can say, for it was now long ago. The mancers, eager to accept their new situation and yet live, were granted the tidbits of knowledge allowed to them. They tell one story, but the wise women tell a different version and perhaps the truth is somewhere in between.

I'm not sure if it matters anymore.

A Foresworn can lie with any woman or man and the child born will be one of them. It is as certain as the rising of the suns. Thus, unlike the mancers, we do not need to worry about the purity of our line. While their legacy withers, ours will endure against time.

Brought into the shadow of the standing rock, Taeor is anchored in place, the chains broken from the ogres and driven into the ground. My father, a firm hand on my shoulder, leads me forward.

The first breaking is the hardest, but as the first child was given to dragons, so must the first now confront them. I remember the words—our secret language known only to those of our blood, alien even to the mancers, who know only the words of docility and contrition.

They envy us in truth. My father told me about Noraan, the last mancer to threaten the Foresworn. Whether he was foolish or simply unable to accept the new order of things, his is a story for another time.

These men bow their heads as we pass, now forbidden to look into the eyes of those whom they would've carried to feed such as the beast huffing and snorting in front of us. We broke our old chains and now make them anew for a different purpose.

I remember the words. They are, after all, a part of my blood.

Taeor shifts his head, rearing as if to spit flame and burn my father and me to ash. At the last moment he stops, head arched back. A tremble warbles the muscle of his thick neck, as though of something building and then guttering into nothing.

His nostrils suck and blow as we come closer, now more or less in his shadow. He knows our scent, and something like a whine rises in his throat.

This close, I can smell the oil dripping from between his scales and the harsh tang of his fire, secreted from the immense sac buried at the base of his neck. I have seen them removed from the dead; the smallest was as large as ten men standing one atop the other.

Another might feel pity to cow a beast such as this, but not I. Father gently nudges me forward; by old law, he can go no further.

My eyes are closed. My hands link together in front of me as the first syllables forge the dragon's chain. Once made, it cannot be broken, linking me to the beast and us both to the past.

My eyes are closed, but I see as Taeor must see. Through the lens of the Neither, he looks impressive, but the aura wrapping him shifts in color. If I was not sure before, I know now he is afraid.

There's an absurdity in there somewhere, in a dragon afraid of a child. We are predators they did not expect, but then, is that not always the case in life?

Someone always proves the stronger in the end.

These creatures are long in our mercy and their debt of blood can never be paid. It must be struck out, one stain at a time, until only we are left standing. So my father said and his before him, and so on and so on and so I will say to my children.

Through the Neither, I feel Taeor's pain for a moment, but only a moment. In its place, I hear the wails of the children taken by those of his own bloodline. So many that their cries merge into a discordant wail.

The wise women say we will find the old ones, the mothers, who have known their children lost to our care. They know, so the old women say, that life as they lived it cannot get any worse.

They are wrong. We have much still to teach them.

Unremembered

A pall hung over London, as it had for ten days. Edwards tried and failed to forget most of the dust was ash, some from buildings and certainly more from people.

The living inhabited the capital like ghosts these days, barely glimpsed as they toiled amid the ruins. A kind of life was returning to the city, though he was not sure exactly what kind.

Most of the bodies are gone, at least. He bit his lip, remembering the scenes around Marble Arch and High Gate.

A soldier and a policeman stopped him near the War Office, now ensconced in an intact townhouse not far from the Thames. He dug out his papers and handed them over.

"Very good, sir," the policeman said and waved him forward.

"Oughtn't you to be in uniform, sir?" asked the soldier.

"I'm not active."

"Your papers beg to differ, sir."

Simmons was reading and pacing when Edwards went into his office.

"Edwards, good."

"Sir."

Simmons dropped the papers to the floor, where they didn't want for company. "Still no uniform, I see."

"Not active, sir."

"We've had this conversation."

You seem to enjoy having it again and again. "I'm a doctor."

"You're whatever I bloody well say you are, and if some sergeant doesn't salute you, I expect you to ball him out for it."

"I'll remember that."

"I doubt it…where's your sense of duty, man?"

"I didn't realize you needed a uniform for that."

"Hmph, I'm surprised your last CO put up with you for as long as he did."

"Depends what you mean by long, sir."

Simmons let it drop. "Take a seat."

Edwards stayed standing. "I've got patients at Shoreditch, sir."

"Take a seat," Simmons repeated. "And anyway, you don't anymore."

"Sir?"

Simmons took out his pipe and started filling it from the pouch resting open on his desk. "Fellow from the Home Office paid me a visit." He struck a match and sucked on the stem. "They need to borrow someone, and I volunteered you."

You enjoy the sound of your own voice, don't you? It was the first thing Edwards had noticed about him.

"I see. Why not Cole or Harris?"

The room slowly filled with the reek of bad tobacco, more acorn and cuttings from the floor than real leaf.

"Cole's taking over from Harris, and Harris is taking Shoreditch."

"You're combining the hospitals?"

"I believe that's what I said." Simmons raised a hand, forestalling more questions. "It's done."

"Alright then. Where am I going, sir?"

"Larkhill, that's all the man would say to me."

"I didn't know there was fighting there."

"Seems no one did, until it was over," Simmons spluttered, sending smoke billowing around his head. "Said you'll be told more when you get there."

"I'm not happy with this, sir."

"Duly noted, now get going. You've a train to catch."

"The line's open?"

"So they tell me."

The warehouse in Shoreditch provided his patients with a degree of comfort and Edwards with a roof over his head and little else, except toil and sleepless nights. He was sad to be leaving it, although Harris was a good doctor.

From the small window in his room, he could see one of the tripods the engineers had yet to bring down. He'd rather grown used to seeing it every day and wondered if it would still be there when he got back.

They should leave it there, so we don't forget.

Of course that wouldn't happen. Not good for the goodwill of the public to see such a thing looming over them.

He imagined someone like Simmons thinking that way from a small office somewhere, then quickly finished his packing.

The train was overfull, all barriers between classes suspended for the duration. Most of those onboard were soldiers, which probably helped to keep the grumbling from escalating further.

Edwards was lucky enough to get a seat without flashing his papers, his valise and doctor's bag were cause enough for people to make way for him. He was too tired to appreciate it much, but was thankful all the same, even if all he could manage was a grunt to show it.

During and since the invasion, he had lived and breathed misery. It had worn him down to a nub, and in quiet moments, he wondered how he was still able to get out of bed.

Doing one's duty, Simmons would've reminded him.

Edwards felt he owed someone something—for surviving, if for nothing else—but if that was duty, it was a million miles from the ideal old men used to gibber on about.

The scenery outside the window flitted past and he settled back, listening to the idle chat of the soldiers as the train rolled on. If not for the gradually receding ruins, he could almost convince himself none of it had happened, provided he closed his eyes.

"Me old lady's been naggin' 'bout our digs."

"Still at the barracks?"

"Wot bleedin' barracks? Ain't much left to speak of."

"Damn near brought it down on us, so they did."

"Engineers…thinkin' man's got no business in uniform."

There were a couple of laughs at this last. Yes, he

could almost believe nothing had happened to the world.

He opened his eyes and saw the wreck of a fallen tripod, its shattered head and body rising above a broken factory close to the tracks.

Almost.

The trains had far fewer stops, passing by towns that had ceased to exist. They made good time because of it.

Larkhill was surprisingly well lit in the oncoming twilight, gas lamps burning softly along the platform as the train pulled in. Some people lingered near the roofless station, mostly soldiers again, but a few civvies here and there.

Edwards hopped off, careful of the gap, and stood on the platform, unsure of who he was supposed to meet. A captain by his pips, tall and gaunt with tired eyes, walked towards him in the company of a shorter man in Donegal tweed.

"Captain Edwards," the shorter of the two said. "I'm Morgan and this is Captain Martins."

Edwards shook the offered hands.

"What did they tell you in London?" Martins asked.

"Not a lot…nothing, in fact."

Morgan looked sidelong at Martins, as if slightly embarrassed. "Sorry about that," he offered.

Edwards wondered what species of the bowler hat brigade Morgan belonged to. "Can either of you tell me why I'm here?"

"It's best if we show you," Martins explained, nodding his head towards a horse and cart manned by a beefy-looking sergeant.

Larkhill had been a garrison town for a long time, but now the barracks had a kind of subdued air about it. Or so it felt to Edwards, at any rate.

Initially, he put it down the invasion, thinking the soldiers here had no doubt seen a good many friends die in it. On the road from town, he'd spied the familiar shape of an upright tripod rising above a wooded hill some distance away. Silhouetted against the twilight, it almost looked to be surveying the area.

"How many are there?"

"Four, though that's the only one still standing," Martins said.

"I'm surprised any of this is left standing." Edwards gestured vaguely as the cart went through the gate.

"They blanketed the place in the Black Smoke," Morgan put in. "Not many got out."

"London wasn't much better."

"We heard," Martins replied. "I was near Manchester when it ended."

"I was trapped in Dover," said Morgan. "Just missed the last ship out of the harbor by about five minutes…shouldn't have expected it any other way. They were dogging us the whole way."

All of us have a story, Edwards thought.

Was London worse than Manchester?

Does it matter? Horror is horror, and all the names on the map can carry epitaphs now.

The sergeant saw to the cart and his bags. Martins'

attitude and bearing changed as they walked across the yard, as though he were uncomfortable in his clothes.

Edwards realized the place wasn't subdued, so much as grimly silent. *Like a grave.*

"If you'll follow us," said Morgan. "We'll show you the infirmary and the reason for the secrecy…I think you'll understand after you see."

There were thirty cots set up along the walls of the arsenal shed, the guns and ammunition cleared out to make room. Most of those in them were men—soldiers—but there were other men and women as well. All were clearly sick.

"Be sure to keep this on," Morgan said, holding a cloth mask up.

Edwards took it and tied it across his face. "What's wrong with them?"

Martins went to a young woman on one of the cots nearest the door. Edwards followed and waited at the foot of the small bed.

She was thin and her skin was waxy, but vividly blotched in places around the neck and jaw. Martins leaned down and gently lifted her left arm up to the light. The girl stirred, but made no other protest. He slid her sleeve down as slowly as he could.

"My god," said Edwards.

Crooked red veins stood out rigidly against her skin, snaking their way down from her wrist and knitting together near her elbow. The hands themselves were clear of the infection, but Edwards noticed they were oddly shaped, as if they were developing too many joints all of a sudden. In the flickering light, they looked a little like claws more than anything else.

Martins motioned him closer, turning the arm to give the doctor a better look.

The shape and pattern of the veins touched a chord in his mind, though he couldn't grasp it. Martins seemed to be waiting for him to say something. Edwards ran his eyes up and down the corrupted limb and stepped back.

"You recognize it, don't you?" asked Morgan.

"That's not all," said Martins. "It's dark, but we have lights to see by."

Escorted by a trio of soldiers, each carrying powerful lamps strapped across their chests, they made their way across the fields by cart. Bright points of light lit up the edge of the wood, and even in darkness, the shadow of the tripod watched them approach.

Edwards reminded himself it was dead, like all the others, and yet somehow this one seemed to retain a shred of life in the night. A young corporal met the cart, saluting Martins as he jumped down.

"Any change?" the captain asked.

"None, sir."

He snapped a finger at the lamp carriers. "Get them on."

The men fumbled with the tapers, and when each caught, the area was bathed in glare as the concave mirrors cast the light back.

"What's in there?" Edwards asked.

"We're far from sure, and god knows what you'll make of it," Morgan offered by way of explanation.

The corporal led them through the trees, and they'd made only a few yards when they came across the first desiccated strands of the Weed.

Edwards had seen it before, but as they carried on, it became darker and more consistent. Soon, he caught glimpses of small red islands surrounded by dry grey. After only a few yards more, it was more or less as red as when it was planted, presumably by the now-dead tripod.

One of the storm lamps shone a beam across a leg, half bent as though caught in midstride. Edwards followed its length upwards before losing it in the branches overhead. The tripod's body was somewhere above them, though he couldn't see it.

He saw the trees themselves were ashen and appeared to be spotted with some kind of mold.

Once past the leg, he saw the first body. Man or woman, it was now impossible to say. Only the shape of outstretched arms and the half-collapsed head could be made out.

By the time he caught sight of the war machine's back, he'd counted out at least twenty he could be sure of, in various poses and states of dissolution. The Weed all around the bodies glistened wetly, while the bodies were as grey and dry as the Weed near the edge of the wood.

"This should be dead by now," Edwards remarked. "It's dead everywhere else."

"We know," said Morgan. "It's no longer growing, but it's not receding either."

"As far as we know, everyone in the infirmary came in contact with this place," Martins added. "Since then, only a few others have fallen ill, and no one else in the last month."

"What about those in contact with the patients?"

Martins shook his head.

"You understand why we had to keep this under wraps?" asked Morgan.

Edwards nodded absently, not yet able to grasp it. He pinched the bridge of his nose and pushed his thumb and forefinger into his eyes, trying and failing to push back the headache he felt coming.

"I think it's best we get back," Martins said. "Dare say you could do with a stiff one."

Edwards couldn't disagree.

The most advanced case was a private named Stephenson. The red veins all but obliterated the features on the left side of his face and blotched one eye a shallow pink. Although he walked with a pronounced shuffle and was unable to use his hands, he was lucid and seemed to be in no serious pain.

"Hello, sir." He managed a smile. "How are you today?"

"Tired, as always. What about yourself?"

"Same, sir." He propped himself on the stool. "Kept up by queer dreams."

Edwards took a syringe out of his bag and drew blood as he had every day in the week and a half since arriving. "What sort of dreams?"

"Can't rightly remember most of them, sir. They just left me with a queer feeling...out of sorts when I woke up."

As soon as he withdrew the needle, the point where it

went in appeared to close. A clear fluid welled up where he'd stuck the patient. Stephenson hadn't so much as flinched or given any sign he'd felt a thing.

"How are your arms doing?"

Stephenson made a show of lifting both as far as his collarbone. Unable to unbend, they looked like gnarled talons. The fingers had too many knuckles.

"Managed to eat without much help today."

"That's something. Turn around, now."

Edwards lifted Stephenson's shirt, exposing his back. The skin here was very far gone. One vein had taken the place of his spine and stood up from the skin, thicker than a man's thumb. Although it looked tough and calloused, the skin was in fact paper-thin and brittle.

Hang it, I need something more.

"Stephenson, I'm going to cut a small sample from here."

"I see, sir. If you have to."

Edwards reached into his bag and removed a long blade. "This will hurt, would you like something for it?"

"Compared to what's already happened to me, I reckon I can deal with a scratch or two."

Morgan read the contents of a leather-bound folio while Martins poured three glasses of brandy. For all that it would be difficult, if not impossible, to replace, he wasn't stingy with the measures.

"The way you describe it here, it's as though you're saying they're undergoing some kind of change," said Morgan, closing the folio.

"It's the only conclusion I can draw…oh, thank you," Edwards said as he took his glass. "Like they're being rewritten from the inside out."

"But not all survive," added Martins. "There were seventy when it started."

"Seventy-five," Morgan corrected.

"I can only account for that with conjecture." Edwards sipped gently from the rim of the glass, then continued. "A lack of compatibility."

It was thin, but a disease from another world only left guesswork when the few open avenues were closed. Their own limited knowledge of the human body only compounded matters.

It all made for a code that could never be broken.

"You don't offer a guess as to what they're being rewritten into," Morgan observed.

Edwards offered nothing and Morgan idly leafed back and forth through the other papers on his desk, one hand fingering the stem of his glass.

"I remembered one of my dreams from the other night, sir."

Edwards listened as he examined Stephenson's right eye. The white was now entirely gone, the color having shifted from its old shallow pink to a red so dark it was almost black. The pupil and iris were impossible to make out clearly, even under the light he held.

"What was it about?" He took the light away and turned his attention to the man's legs.

"It sort of came back in bits and pieces. I was on sand

and it was that strange orangey-red color, like clay or light rust."

"Ochre."

"Knew you'd know it, bein' an educated man, sir. Anyway, I was standing in this place and there weren't nothing for miles and miles." Stephenson frowned for a moment before continuing. "Only I could hear a sound on the wind, and I'd heard it before and didn't want to hear again."

"Go on, it might be important," Edwards urged, suspecting the sound Stephenson described was one he too was familiar with.

"I felt something, sir…like I belonged there."

Morgan walked with him, the pair smoking vicious-tasting, hand-rolled cigarettes.

"Who are you, Morgan?" Edwards asked.

"I don't quite follow."

Edwards all but heard the unsaid 'old boy' catch in his throat. "I mean, which den in Whitehall do you call your own…what kind of creature are you?"

Morgan considered the question, drew in smoke, and answered on the exhale. "The kind one seldom sees."

"That clears that up, then."

"I'm sorry."

Edwards realized later he wasn't apologizing for his obliqueness.

Sunday evening near dark found the yard space taken up by a newly arrived group of carts. Enough to carry a platoon, Edwards judged. The sergeant-in-charge pointed him inside the main building.

Entering the office, he found Morgan and Martins joined by a third man. Even with his back to him, Edwards recognized Simmons straight away.

"Come to collect me?"

Simmons slowly turned to face him, and Edwards noticed the look Martins and Morgan shared.

"Captain, Mr. Morgan, would you be so kind as to step outside for a moment?"

Both did, closing Edwards in with Simmons. The room was utterly still, save for their breathing. Before Simmons could speak, Edwards did.

"You're anxious to know if this disease can spread?" he asked, guessing Simmons had been reading the reports he'd filed and Whitehall had sent him.

His chief didn't answer, but moved his hands for Edwards to continue.

"I'd have to say it's caused by some sort of change in the Weed near the tripod." He sat heavily and rubbed his eyes. "However it happened, the Weed changed and spored. Some mixing of biology perhaps and it infected those who came into contact."

"Are you sure?"

"I can't be, but it makes sense and it explains why no one else has been infected. The spores are dead, and the process that made them seems no longer to be happening."

"But there were other cases after the initial infection, right up until about a month ago."

"Sporadic, a leftover from the initial sporing...if that

is what happened."

Being in Simmons' presence drained Edwards of the energy he had left. Surprisingly, Simmons filled two glasses from Martins' much-reduced brandy bottle and offered one to the doctor. Edwards had always thought the man a teetotaler.

"You needn't have brought those men outside."

"Orders from Whitehall."

Simmons gulped loudly at his brandy, the sign of a nervous or unpracticed drinker.

"The Home Office have read all your reports and it seems clear your patients are changing into something…I wanted to hear it from you, exactly what they're becoming."

Edwards pushed out a breath and sat back. "I really can't say until it's seen through to the end."

"I'd like it very much if you could do your best."

Edwards didn't want to confront the answer the facts pointed to. Thinking it was one thing, saying it quite another. "Something like a hybrid between us and them, and that's assuming all of them survive the process." He laid the untouched drink on the table near his chair. "I've no idea how long it will take for that to happen."

"But it will?"

"It has to, or kill them in the attempt."

"Can it be reversed?"

"No."

"And those who do survive?"

"Will no longer be human."

Simmons tipped the last of his brandy down his throat, stood, and went to the door. Edwards rose to follow him, but was stopped when Simmons held his hands up.

"No, you stay here for a spell. You look about done in."

Edwards awoke with no memory of nodding off. Morgan sat behind the desk, staring at the blotter.

"Thought it best to let you catch a few winks."

"Thank you."

"It's a bad business, this."

"I've had patients I couldn't help before, but nothing like this."

"No. This is different, though, isn't it?" Morgan got up and stood by the window behind the desk. Out of sight, the dead tripod was looking back at them. "It's easy to forget how delicate things are," he said. "Here, it feels as if things are getting back to normal, however slowly."

"Maybe, but I know people in Shordeitch who would argue with you."

"Abroad, though, that's where a crack or two could appear if things fall apart here, and then we'll have no chance of getting back on our feet." Morgan turned to look at him. "You were in the army overseas, so you take my meaning?"

"I do, but I don't like it."

"Oh?"

"Our way of doing things has a way of breaking people."

Morgan's face was calm.

From outside, a racket of hooves on stone and creaking axels reached the window. There were voices thrown into the mix, shouts and barked orders. Edwards understood their meaning, if not the content.

"We can't have a panic, not now, and we can't let this get out," Morgan began. "You said yourself that it can't be reversed."

Edwards ran for the door and threw himself down the stairs. Two armed men took hold of him as soon as he made it outside; beyond them, the gates were held fast. Eventually, they let him go, but he stayed in the yard and stared towards where the wooded hill and the tripod were.

From so far away, the shots sounded like firecrackers, robbing them of lethality. They rolled over each other until they stopped.

After a few minutes, a flash winked in the distance and soon flared up, under-lighting the tripod so more of it stood out, even from so far away. The fire spread fast and was clearly visible by the time the carts trundled back through the gates.

Each was empty, save for the soldiers.

Mods and Rockers

The winter market was where it'd always been, in front of the Rathaus on Museumplatz. Now it was dwarfed by spires of black glass and nano-recombinated steel. It wasn't quite as dazzling as it had been in the last century.

Holograms strobed across the old stonework and leapt into the air, where they morphed and roiled into fractals. The jockeys were lost in the crowd; working their consoles anonymously, save to themselves. Each 'cast was a bespoke "fuck you" from one to another.

Lisa wasn't interested in their game, she'd seen it often enough to know it for the pissing contest it was. I did too, but I stole a glance now and then.

A Mod leaned against the counter of a nearby kiosk, holding forth to two girls in plastic raincoats. They gave him their undivided attention, which suggested they weren't from Vienna.

Tourists ate up the local wildlife and what they put on show. In his case, it was a pair of black doll eyes and chameleon-skin grafts, the color of which he changed in time with the overhead holo-casts.

He had a decent degree of control. I gave him that much.

"Wondering how much he spent on that?" Lisa asked casually.

"Not really." I could have told her how much it would cost, but there was no point. "If they're into it, good for them."

"You don't approve of entertaining the tourists?"

"I don't approve of easily impressed idiots."

"You were one."

"Times change."

Drooling over the displays in the graft-shops and 'ware stalls had lost its appeal a while back. I *was* modified, but in a very different fashion from the show-off across the way.

Lisa tapped my arm and showed me where to look with her eyes.

A stocky Mod with bone and muscle grafts bulking him up pushed his way through the crowd. Most of them managed to get out of the way, but a few couldn't, and I caught the beginnings and endings of a score of possible fights.

"Now?"

"No." I moved closer to her, almost in a clinch and the cover of assumed intimacy.

Muscle-fiber bundles stood out on his neck, tugging at the carbon plates filling out his chest. They were showy, but functional. The carbon and fiber bundles were woven together for fluidity of movement. He was almost on top of the other Mod, who was still busy impressing his audience.

"Now."

Lisa stepped back and flicked up the collar of her jacket. She dilated and shimmered before vanishing, a slight bending of the air the only sign of her passing.

"Hey!" Muscles shouted.

The other Mod turned in mild irritation, looked about

to say something, but stopped short. The girls chose that moment to duck out. The gun he'd produced in his hand had robbed his previous display of its interest.

A wire-thin flash sparked briefly, just kissing his hand. The muscles tightened, causing his trigger finger to squeeze.

The angle was good. The gun barked and blew out Muscle's throat, spraying those closest with a mist of dark blood.

There was a moment of silence before someone screamed and the crowd nearby surged in panic. I let myself be carried away with them and lost sight of Lisa's shimmer.

I wasn't concerned. She'd show at Leopoldstadt sooner or later, and I was content to cool my heels for her.

Tonight had been easy to engineer. A few words dropped in the right ear would pass down a chain that had no idea where the story had originated, and with each telling, the story would be embellished.

I knew how to play them. I'd been one of them.

Crossing the river, it's called now. Going over. Defection, whatever name suits you. I did it, but not through choice.

It's a rare thing, because if the other side is unreceptive, you can end up as bits washing up along the banks of the Danube. If you're not so lucky and your side catches you, it's worse. I'd seen Mods have their grafts and 'ware ripped out just for talking about it.

I did some of it. I didn't know any better.

Sometimes, though, you can't see the ground rushing up at you until it's too late.

Hannes had something for me. Call it a crush, but he wasn't my type and I gave him the brush off when I found out.

Don't get me wrong, he was cute, but also immature and vain and carrying enough daddy issues to fill a bulk hauler. Most of his grafts went towards making him look pretty and gradually more androgynous.

I didn't care too much when he drifted to Josef. They suited each other. A vain child and a narcissist craving worship.

Of course, that wasn't how Hannes saw it.

Liesing was well beyond the river, but boundaries never stopped the Rockers from strolling over. They respected no marker, line, or tag. They'd been around since before the last war.

Polezei drone barriers flashed and drawled their warnings to a small knot of people around an old factory. Two Mods were crucified on the wall with what looked iron rails driven into their hands and shoulders.

From where I stood, I saw their implants were in place. Not worth the effort. A sign designed to provoke.

Lacking any obvious modification, I was just another face taking a peek at some excitement.

"Move back," an amplified voice ordered at the same time lights stabbed down from a descending *polezei* cruiser.

The onlookers shuffled off reluctantly, and I copied their pace.

I met Lisa for the first time there, but didn't know her from any of the other gawkers. She brushed past my shoulder, just close enough to draw my attention. Our eyes met for a second, and then she was gone with the rest as the cruiser touched down.

Hannes opened the door on my third knock. From the look of his eyes, I could see he was on the needles tonight and no fucking use to anyone.

"Lol," he said.

I ground my teeth and wondered why he couldn't just laugh. "Right." I stepped around him and into the old gallery.

"Fancy one?"

"No," I said as I looked around. "Where's Flori?"

"Out." He'd produced a thumb-sized needle from somewhere and was busy trying to find a clean vein. "Josef's back soon."

"I need Florian."

"Guess you'll be waiting, then."

"Guess I will."

He made a sound in his throat and flopped down on an old beanbag. I stayed standing and looked around as much as I could, knowing that to make eye contact with him in this state was asking for an argument I could do without.

He started tossing needle after needle across the room, one or two coming close to hitting my shins. I ignored it. A headache came on gradually and a clot of rusty-tasting spit was gathering at the back of my throat.

I won't lie; I started it.

"Those things'll ruin your pretty complexion."

Hannes snorted. "Why are you so fucking uptight?

Too clean for the rest of us, bitch?"

About what I expected. "Born that way, I suppose."

"Thought as much."

"Didn't stop you wanting, did it?" I was surprised when he didn't answer, so I pushed. "Happy with Josef?"

The look on his face was one I hadn't seen before, and I put it down to the amount of shit he'd shot up. I put my back to him, contenting myself with the far wall in the next room.

A loose board creaked behind me. When I turned, he was close enough to touch, his hands already reaching for my waist.

"No," he mumbled.

I took his hands. "No, what?"

"No, I'm not happy with Josef."

He pushed against my grip, trying to take handfuls of my jacket and t-shirt where he could.

"Stop."

"No, no I don't want to."

"You're fucked."

"Not yet." He smiled a high kind of smile and stretched his neck out to bring his lips onto mine.

"No, for fuck's sake!"

A stress response can trigger a gland, a graft, or a piece of 'ware without meaning to. Depends on how wired in it is. I tell myself that's what must have happened, because I threw him back with enough force to crack his skull open on the edge of a stone table.

My ears rang and my throat burned with the effort of breathing. A hand near his mouth and the extent of the injury told me what I already knew.

"Oh fuck, fuck fuck *fuck!*"

I turned on the spot, looking for who knows what, and saw a pair of eyes glinting from the landing above the wall I'd been looking at just minutes, or years it seemed, before.

I ran.

Mods don't kill Mods, not without a proper reason, and an unrequited crush doesn't count. Punishment killings are worse for breaking this rule. They leave you intact enough to die by degrees.

It didn't matter who was up there on the landing. Before long, everyone who mattered would know.

Before long, I realized I was walking in the direction of the river. Gradually, I slowed. I'd already crossed one kind of bridge tonight, but a more fundamental one held all manner of other possibilities.

Go back, see how it plays out.

Sounded reasonable. I could plead my case. He was high, and it got a bit out of hand. An accident.

On my knees in the gallery with a crowd watching, practically tasting the blood even before the cutting started.

Would I scream?

Probably.

Would I beg?

Everyone tries not to, usually without success.

I might survive.

Now you're just being stupid.

I checked the time. Almost midnight. All Saints Day

in a few minutes. *Polezei* would be in Innere Stadt, the Riesenrad, and Prater. Not a guarantee, but better than the certainty behind me.

For the first time in ages, I wanted a hit. I settled for a plastic bottle of slivovice instead and carried on my way.

Rockers can pass for un-modded, whereas most of the time, we can't. It's easily their most useful method, allowing them to blend into the fabric of the city and slip between the various claimed districts. There were places where they could be found, though, and I was fairly sure I'd heard that one or two bars around the Prater belonged to them.

Lisa would advise me later to "Brass it out," and I like to think I did a pretty good job.

I walked in and sat down at a table. Across the way, two *polizei* cruisers sat idling. Glancing around, I saw the more obvious stares and the not-so-obvious. No one I wanted was here; when the nudge came, I wouldn't know about it until someone took the seat opposite.

It was a middle-aged man who finally sat down. He wore a tweed jacket, and his hair was slicked and parted in the middle.

"Sure you're in the right place?"

"Pretty sure."

He waved a finger at the waiter, who'd done a good job of pretending I wasn't there. He arrived a moment later, carrying a tray with two beers.

"You're not very stupid," he said, sipping his beer and glancing over my shoulder towards the cruisers. "But they won't help you."

"Didn't have time to think of anything else to do."

"Heard there was some dust-up across the river." He flashed a smile. "Mods are on the warpath, so I hear."

I was tired of the preamble, but didn't feel I could do anything except bear it.

"You angling to come over?" he asked at last.

"Yes."

"Why us and not someone else?"

I didn't feel I could lie. He was probably wired to detect changes in body temperature and to read voice fluctuations. "I don't know, it was the first thought I had."

He didn't seem surprised by the answer, only nodded and pushed his beer away. When he got up, I went with him.

There were no guarantees, but it was better than nothing. If nothing else, he'd bought me a drink before killing me, which was more than my old set would've done.

Tweedy left me in a windowless room at the back of a suite of bare cubicles near the edge of the Prater.

I couldn't hear anything through the thin-looking walls, so nothing would leak out if they were going to kill me. I still think that was the plan all along, but I've no proof and I haven't raised it with anyone since.

The reason I think so is because after Lisa arrived, there was a palpable change in things. She walked in through the door and recognized me straight away.

"You," she said slowly, "are in the shit, from what I hear."

"Thanks for your support."

"Anytime."

I slid the half-finished bottle of slivovice from my jacket pocket and took a swig. She waited until I was finished before holding her hand out. I handed it over, and she took a small swallow before continuing.

"You feel like telling me why you did it?"

"Lover's tiff."

She nodded and took another drink. "C'mon."

I got the impression if I asked her where we were going, she'd tell me not to be so dense. So I kept quiet and forgot to ask for the flask back, only remembering when she dropped it into a waste bin along the way.

I'm too young to remember Landstrasse before the war. The Belvedere and its gardens were a covered market then—and still are. The stalls were built up around the water basin, which had survived where the old palace had not.

Only high-end graftees came here, ruling it out for the majority of the city. Still, it was busy and had the kind of rustic look the rich seemed to appreciate.

"The Flesh Market," Lisa said. "You've heard of it?"

"We have a different name for it, across the river."

"I'm sure you do."

A black steel cube rested on raised legs above the water, connected by a wireframe walkway. I followed her over and noticed the chemical clean smell in the air for the first time.

Surgical, the word almost made it to my tongue.

The old man was Mongolian, but the clutch of

mechanical arms rising out from his back put me in mind of a spider. While he tinkered with some glass slides, the arms moved like they had a mind of their own—picking things up, putting them down somewhere else, and tapping keys on consoles.

"Taskhia," said Lisa.

The arms turned towards us before he did.

He could have been fifty or a hundred. Taskhia walked with little rushed steps, the mechano-arms folding neatly behind him as he came closer.

"Doctor, if you please."

"Sorry, Doctor." She gestured my way and stepped aside.

Four lenses clicked one over the other across his right eye as he looked me up and down. I could see tiny characters stream down the glass, reversed and impossible for me to read even if they were in a language I knew.

"Hmmm, we can do something with this one."

"Like open me up?"

"Oh and more besides."

"Last chance to turn back," Lisa reminded me. "For all you know, you won't come back up after he puts you under."

I looked from her to him.

Tskhia's mechano-arms unfurled, regarding me like a gaggle of hungry birds.

"What did they do?"

Lisa arrived an hour after I did. After the crowd surge ebbed, I'd taken a roundabout way to Leopoldstadt, thinking she'd be there before me.

"You didn't know them?"

"No."

"Killed a supplier who wouldn't sell to them."

"The way it happened, it'll look like an out-of-hand feud. Not that that will save the poser."

"You hung up about what they'll do to him?"

I was, but not in any serious way.

"Just seeing if you were."

Up Over Geary

Jan brought the skiff towards the beach. The sun was setting as I watched him approach, bathing the still water of the sound in gold.

My grandfather could've probably remembered a time when the buildings under the water had stood taller than what I lived in now. All I knew came from stories before the quakes, and all I'd lived had been otherwise.

The tallest buildings anywhere on the archipelago were on the Escarpment. Even they weren't more than three or four storeys at most—and so packed together that they were holding each other up like drunks.

When he was close enough, Jan hopped over the side and pushed the skiff the rest of the way up onto the shingle. I helped him haul it a little further when he looked to be giving up.

"Anything?"

He lifted a bag from the boat and shook it, a smile splitting his tanned face. He nodded back across the water, where the low shape of Sutron was backlit by the descending sun.

"Where first?" he asked, still smiling. "Judah? Sunset or the Shores?"

I wasn't supposed to meet Marush for a few hours yet, so I figured we had time enough to hit a couple of places before I had to duck out.

"Sunset sounds good," I said, deciding it was close

enough to the Shores so I wouldn't have to worry.

"Atahan's?"

I nodded and helped him fasten the tarpaulin over the skiff, then made sure it was anchored for tide change when it came.

Sunset was basically the Escarpment in miniature, if that was possible.

Single as opposed to multi-storey buildings, and only about half the size. The Highlands loomed above it and its lights, many of which pulsed and blazed different colours. They seemed to draw half the archipelago every night.

Jan slipped out of his shorts in the back of the buggy and pulled on a pair of dark combats. I'd dressed before, already knowing somewhere in the back of my mind what I would say when he got back with the buy.

Even with autumn on the turn, the night was still mild and people were gathering along the roads and paths on their way into town.

"Wonder if Sunna and Nela are here?" Jan asked.

"Probably. Marek too, most likely."

"Shame he doesn't float my way." Jan patted my leg.

"I don't float your way, Jan, and it's a little early for that."

"Sometimes you're no fun, Zack."

It wasn't my name, but I'd worn it long enough that it felt utterly familiar.

"I try."

Sunna was chatting to a young Chinese guy, a lit

cigarette between the fingers of her right hand. The terrace was packed, and I was surprised they were able to hold a conversation. I was more surprised to hear him answer in perfect Farsi when I was close enough.

I shouldn't have been, not really, but something twinged tight and almost snapped my head around in the process. I let it go by raising my eyebrows.

In the years since the quakes on the west coast, the world had become more and more globalised—if that was possible. It wasn't unusual to hear a dozen and more languages in one night at Atahan's.

He gave me one glance, quick, like he was nervous or only acting like he was. I wasn't sure and I was trying to let go of whatever I was feeling, because it was uncomfortable to feel it again after so long. Old, worn-down parts of myself trying to jam themselves back into the spaces they'd occupied. It happened a few times in a year.

He said his goodbyes to Sunna and joined another group at the other end of the terrace. He looked to be mingling and then was lost in the crowd. I put him out of my mind.

"Not going after your friend?" I asked, almost having to shout to make myself heard.

"Nah," she said and blew smoke before offering me a cigarette. "He was a little too intense."

I left the three of them after sinking a few vodkas and hired a bike from a kiosk on the next street. It was just after eleven, and the moon peered out occasionally from behind the clouds. At this time of night, the tracks were more or less empty, most people having made the exodus to the hotspots hours before.

Marush was a creature of habit. He would be half an hour early and he would wait no more than thirty minutes the other side of that. I had plenty of time.

My cheeks burned hot and cold as I sped along close to the shore. A chill breeze kicked up from the surf and I blinked tears out of my eyes from time to time.

Out across the water, I saw the 'scraper come into view. Now it was a lighthouse. I'd never met anyone who could tell me what the building had been before—and probably no one would've cared anyway.

The old San Francisco only existed in books or online now.

I made a turn down a smaller, narrower path and worked the throttle hard. The bag on my back weighed almost nothing, and I had to keep reminding myself it was still there.

There'd been a time when I wouldn't have needed to, but that was before. Now, I was just as fallible as everyone else—or so I kept telling myself.

Letting go isn't easy, but I thought I'd done a pretty good job of it.

The bike's engine block ticked as the metal cooled. Out of habit, I left it under a stand of stunted trees and climbed down to the beach.

The Shores is home to straggling shanties that snake and wind along the steep hills. People come here to buy and sell. If the Escarpment and Peninsula are the seats of power, then the Shores is the free market of the archipelago.

The climb wasn't hard, but I slid and stumbled more than anything else, falling into a heavy-footed run on the last part of the slope.

Matush was nowhere to be seen. At first, I thought he might be walking a trail along the beach.

Something old and rusty through lack of use started to click into place in the back of my mind. It happened so slowly that I almost didn't realise it until I noticed I was clenching and unclenching my hands like how I used to before an op.

I reached the water line, understanding the pattern of footprints I'd picked up on even from ten meters away. On the surface, they were nothing special to look at, but I could read the story they had to tell.

Stopping, I knelt and peered at the dark patch on the sand, which was almost invisible in the dark. It might have been dismissed as a shadow or just a splash of water.

A lot of old responses—hard-wired, but jerky—came back.

I turned a little awkwardly, in time to see the first black-clad figure coming towards me in a crouched jog. He was already within five meters. In the past, I suppose I would've heard him, despite the roar of the surf.

The bag was off my back in an easy shrug and then sailing through the air towards him. There was a cough as a silenced weapon fired, the shot clipping the bag, but not enough to divert it.

He had to raise his rifle to bat it away, giving me the opening I needed. Stepping past the barrel, I twisted the gun free of his grip, bringing the business end up under his chin.

My thumb found his finger and pressed. This close, the weapon sounded no louder than it had before, but there was a distinct wet thwack as the bullet went up through his head.

The rifle was pressed into my shoulder before he hit the ground, in time for the other two—already close enough for me to reach out and almost touch.

Time crawled, as if I was watching them through a slow-motion capture. Something burned the air next to my right cheek and grazed my ear. There wasn't any kick, and only when they fell did I realise I'd already fired, which explained why the shot went wide from so close.

Time returned to something like its normal rate, and I felt my legs start to tremble as the muscles misfired on the cocktail of stimulants pumping into them. A hard, metallic taste crept to the back of my throat, and I spat in a vain effort to clear it.

Only three?

Lucky, I guess.

Kneeling, I reached for the closest body and pulled back the mask of his full-body whisper suit. The face staring blankly up at me had skin too smooth and featureless.

Probably from a vat, they always were ten a penny. Keep 'em in stasis until needed. Not like that narrows it down.

There were no distinguishing marks, aside from a small bar code behind his right ear. Without a medical scanner, it meant nothing.

Part of me had always thought something like this was going to happen, but it had slipped somewhere along the way. Not entirely, or else there's no way I would've been able to deal.

After de-mob, it had been difficult to let the rational part of my mind come to the fore again. When it had, I thought the archipelago was as diverse a place as any on the Rim to get lost in.

I emptied his smart webbing without looking away from the smooth, almost boyish face. My hands looked on their own for the old, familiar shapes, and I carried the haul to where the bag had landed.

Slinging the rifle and the now-heavier pack, I started back up the slope towards the bike.

"No, the four of them left," the waiter explained. He didn't say anything about the gun hanging off my shoulder—weapons were common enough that no one paid them much attention.

The fourth person could've been anyone. On any other night, it probably would've been. Not tonight. The Chinese guy had gone with Jan and the girls, and I knew I was never going to see them again.

It was possible he had nothing to do with any of this, but putting it all together was like finding an old and favourite toy to play with after years spent thinking it was lost.

He marked me, probably low-cast comms bead and a sub-vocal radio. Something I would miss, because I didn't look.

I started walking, knowing I was in all likelihood being watched, but without much of a choice to do anything else.

It's what's expected, play to it.

If someone expects you to do something, then it sometimes pays off not to disappoint.

The burn in my muscles had transmuted into a searing ache. Old micro-chem shunts still pumping by now semi-toxic shit into places where they hadn't been known in an age. The pain lent clarity, giving me something to hold onto.

Assume they know everyone who knows you. Make a list of hardest to access to the easiest.

The list wasn't long. It didn't mean anything, but it was all I had to work with—and I'd been taught to work with a lot less. Ducking into a gap between a strip club and a fighting pit, I broke open the bag.

The bullet had passed through the top, missing the packets Jan had brought over from Sutron what felt like ten years ago at that moment. Andexaphin would take the edge off the worst pain and do something to straighten out the bio-ware. We'd used its precursor during induction, although I had no idea what kind of shit this had been cut with.

Dry-swallowing three, I picked up both bag and rifle and cut into the warren of alleys that made up most of Sunset

Potrero and Bernal are the official entry points for the archipelago.

The small nest of wharfs, piers, and the ugly landing field at Russian Point presented a much harder prospect for illegal entry or exit. Everything illicit came and went through there, and only those with the hardest of hard currency were given the time of day.

It was a standing joke that the black port maintained harder entry requirements than the official security and check-in desks.

Hard currency meant either euros, old dollars, or pan-pacific credits, none of which I had to hand. There was a stash back at my shack, but that was playing too much to expectations.

I wasn't up for a trek across the island in my current state. I was coming up, but the drug was interacting in a fucked-up way with my own 'ware and I wasn't sure how many more I could risk dropping. I figured I'd end up necking quite a lot of the packet before the night was done.

I trusted to my list that at least one name on it hadn't been done in already.

The bike's battery was about done, and given the whine rising in pitch with every turn of the throttle, I doubted it would make it much farther. The chance of finding a spare fuel cell was about nil; people tended to hang onto those when they got them.

I left it behind in a small gulley and walked the rest of the way.

Putting one foot in front of the other with a weight on my back brought back a lot of memories from induction and basic. It brought more clarity than I thought I needed.

Grief would only come after I closed my eyes. The conditioning turned loss into anger, but in sleep, it surged up from wherever it was dumped and filled my head with dreams I could never shake.

Anger was the fuel for the cold detachment settling in

behind my eyes, spreading out from the coldest depths of my mind. A place I had thought, though never truly believed, was entirely dead.

We all have that cold part in us. We like to imagine it isn't there, until one day it is.

It's funny, but only as I walked through the bushes, past the remains of overgrown buildings, did I realise the Tutors had been right after all. None of what had been done to me could be taken away. It might have frayed about the edges, but it was still there—still coiled around my spinal cord and central nervous system.

None of us had believed them at the time.

I mean how could they know…I mean, really *know?* The tech was still so new that sixty percent of the inductees rejected the implants and conditioning both. The lucky ones died.

Only after Bardejov and de-mob did the problems and side effects become apparent. Stories about gees going off the deep end or going through a much more prolonged rejection later in life. Even when Sofia—I knew her—ate her gun one night in a bar in a Fukoka slum, I remained unconvinced.

Everything before tonight was play acting. I hated it, because it made everything I'd built here into a lie with the throw of a stupid fucking bag.

It still felt like coming home.

An osprey banked overhead. I was in cover three heartbeats before its shadow passed over me. I'd dropped a couple of more pills and the shunts and glands seemed to be tightening up. Parts of the conditioning were snapping whipcord tight.

How long can you keep propping everything up with sub-standard, stepped-on shit?

Sub-standard was a relative term. In this case, it only meant what my nervous system was used to in a previous life. That being said, I knew the voice was right. I was on the clock before I became septic in a major way or one of my organs failed. I already felt something like steel wool worrying its way under the skin of my arms.

Ahead, I spied the lights of the landing field and the faint shimmer of the security barrier.

Without thinking, the rifle slid into my hands. The sound of the seeker drone became clear a moment later. The osprey's engine had masked it, but I'd still caught it at the edge of hearing.

My first shot blew out its image catcher and the second followed through, blowing out the internal mechanisms and sending it tumbling to the ground. Still too late.

They could have teams anywhere on the island, although more likely there was a trio of gunships orbiting somewhere, ready to move when the drones found something. They could cross the archipelago in less than ten minutes.

"You're a gee?" Hillard finally asked after I'd told him.

"Saying it for a second time isn't going to make it any less real."

"Sorry, just processing." He puffed on a cheroot and

topped up his coffee from the vodka bottle near his hand. "Saw some of you guys once, near Baku."

"I wasn't there."

"No?"

"No, close though. Central and Eastern Europe mostly. Some ops on the Black Sea." *You're wasting time on memory lane.* "Can you take me or not?"

"I can take, but it'll cost."

I dropped one pack of pills on the table between us. "That cover it?"

Hillard slid it towards him gently, hefted it, and tossed it from one hand to the next. "Should, but what the Russians?"

I already knew what I was going to offer them.

"Get me there. After that, I'm no longer your responsibility."

Hillard's osprey was an out-of-date vector thrust model, and climbing into it brought back a wash of sudden memory.

Outside Krakow as the city burned behind us.

Skirting over the Visegrad perimeter near Kosice. Pillars of smoke rising as grave markers for tanks and striders; so many, they blotted out the sun. Ours or theirs? Impossible to say.

Hillard tapped me on the shoulder, a comm bead and mic in one hand.

"So, these guys who're after you," he said as the engines flared, vibrating the floor of the cockpit so hard I thought my teeth would break.

"No idea," I said, adjusting the mic. "Could be anyone."

There was a pregnant pause, noticeable over the rising scream of the engines. I saw a miniscule shift in his body language and a twinge in his complexion.

I was going to come down hard after firing on so many cylinders for so long.

"What?" I almost snapped.

"When I was in Baku, we had some special forces types along for a ride with us," he said. "You know the type…pricks with wraparound sun shades."

I nodded.

"They said after the war, someone was going to pull the trigger on you guys. Said you'd be tidied up in the end, no matter how well you served your country."

"You believe that?"

"Not until tonight."

The thought had occurred that one day the fuckers who'd done this to me might clip those of us left over. The immediate will to clean up hadn't been there after Bardejov.

Wait for the conditioning and mods to finish some. Minus those lost in combat. Find and retire the rest.

That was what they called it when one of us 'malfunctioned' in the field: retirement.

They got us to do it to our own.

I'd done it twice without saying anything. One of us went bad, and he or she had to go. It was pretty simple— and it didn't matter if you said no, because someone else would do it and probably throw you against the wall too.

Neither one said a single word before I pulled the

trigger, but for some reason, that isn't how I remember it.

Russian Point sprawls across a small island that the locals call Chierna Ostrov. Most of it was still covered in tarmac, which the Russians repaired all the time as a kind of marker.

Black Island.

The osprey's threat alarm suite lit up as we came in. Hillard swore and flicked the controls and switches in an order that looked totally random to me.

After twenty very long seconds, the lights returned to green.

"Fuck me," he breathed. "They know my IFF."

"That shouldn't have happened?"

He shook his head.

They probably knew something about what was up tonight, but maybe not the full story. That would make my job easier or more difficult, depending on how jumpy they were.

We were still flying, which I took for a good sign.

Hillard idled long enough to drop me, and then took off again. He gave me a small wave, which I returned. My weapon and bag were taken as soon as the osprey was clear, and I was 'escorted' inside.

Two men led me across the field to a bunker, which partly rose up from the ground like a half-buried barrel. Inside, it was lit by a couple of glow strips, long since past their use-by date. All the others had peeled off, leaving lighter patches of concrete in their wake.

I didn't know the two men waiting for me inside, one sitting and the other standing, but I knew who they were.

Sasha and Radovan ran the port like a fiefdom. No one was prepared to argue the toss with them about it. Their bosses on the mainland gave them a lot of freedom, as long as they made money along the way.

I slid out a metal chair from under my side of the table without waiting for them to offer, but neither seemed to mind. Sasha nudged his partner, who grumbled something and took down a flat flask of vodka from its perch on a filing cabinet.

"Not everyone who comes in unannounced gets such a friendly welcome," said Sasha. He opened the flask and tipped it to his lips.

"Well, at this point, any way off the archipelago would be nice." I took the flask and swallowed a measure. It was shit, but I didn't show anything.

"You look a little cash-poor at the moment, my friend," said Radovan. "We're not really into the charity side of things."

"I'd thought as much."

"My friend raises a point...we're not into freebies."

"Money's not the hardest currency going these days."

"Pretty solid, last time we checked," Radovan said with a cold smile.

I pointed at my chest.

They didn't look at each other in surprise. So they both knew what I was—or had an idea, at least.

"What's to stop us from killing you and breaking you down into spare fucking parts," Sasha asked, not entirely unkindly.

"Won't work."

"No?" Radovan sneered.

"No."

They were far from ignorant, so it was a question of just how far their ignorance went and how much they would swallow of what I gave to them.

"If you kill me, my body will release protein markers. They'll spoil me so nothing can be harvested."

"We could simply drug you," Sasha offered.

"You could try."

We stared at each other for a while, until I reached for the flask. "I don't suppose either of you have a cigarette?"

Sasha produced a packet and tossed it across, along with a cheap plastic lighter. I teased one out and lit it.

"There's a long list of drugs and nerve agents I can't be exposed to without the same thing happening." I brushed my hands along my torso. "Chemical dermals pop and I die."

"What do you suggest?" Sasha asked.

That was fifty percent down. Subtle tells in his face told me more than he could say with words.

"You can use a local anaesthetic. That way, I'll be able to tell your people where to go and what to look for."

"We could just kill you after," said Radovan.

"True, and that's entirely up to you, but I like to think what I'm offering is worth a hop over the water."

"Depends." Radovan lit a cigarette he produced from somewhere. "We hear the kind of people following you are a little on the serious side," he said as he blew smoke at me.

"It's why the port's locked down."

Their idea about what a lock-down meant didn't quite meet the standard I was used to. That being said, I wasn't about to offer advice.

Move the show along, now.

Radovan's hand went to his thigh holster as soon as I stood. I saw the trajectory the table would take if I put my foot into it at a certain angle. There'd be enough force behind it to ensure it broke when it hit them both, my own foot included.

I wouldn't feel it anyway, so it was still a win-win, at least until someone kicked the door in behind me. Then moving fast could become an issue.

It all happened in less than a second, but Sasha was up fast—though to me, he moved incredibly slowly. I read his intention and relaxed a fraction. He put his hand on Radovan's and whispered something hard and hissing into his ear.

"Alright," he said. "How long will it take?"

"A couple of hours." I stepped back out of reach of the table, as big a sign of trust as I could manage right then. "And I want one more thing."

"Fuck—" Radovan started, before Sasha cut him off dead.

"What?"

"Zadarin."

"What for?"

"My own use, and you'll need to pack the samples in a solution made from it."

I could practically hear his mind turning quickly over.

It didn't take long, because one set of numbers came to a greater total than the other.

"Once you're off the island, you're on your own."

I nodded, and we shook hands.

Maybe if I'd an idea about where different parts of me were going to end up, I might've thought twice. But that's something I only tell myself at night.

Tin Soldiers

Arms gripped him, holding him down against the stretcher. He imagined this was how men led to the wall to be shot must feel, conducted unwillingly to the spot.

He sympathised. The same was true in his case.

Vaguely, he tried to make a fist of his right hand. Anything to stop the pain, but the effort only made it worse. Lifting his head, he saw the mangled remains of his right arm flopping uselessly in time with the motion of the stretcher.

"Hold him down," someone said, and his head was gently pushed back so he stared up at the passing lights above.

His journey on the stretcher came to an end and he felt himself being lifted onto a much firmer bed. More hands touched his body, starting to cut away the tatters of his uniform.

Cold, strong-smelling liquid is squirted over his chest and rubbed across it with something soft. Turning his head, he looked again at the mangled wreck of his right arm.

He couldn't decide if it should hurt more or if it hurt enough for the state of it. A face appeared next to his own, half hidden by a surgical mask.

"Captain, we're going to have to remove your arm."

"No," his voice was almost a whisper.

"We have no choice."

"No." He thought it sounded more emphatic that time.

The face withdrew, and he heard someone say, "Large-bore syringe, ten milligrams morphia. Nurse, prepare the bone saw."

"No."

"No!" Yanos opened his eyes and stopped himself from jerking upright, knowing from experience the pain it would cause in his side and back.

Slowly, he got his breathing under control and made a fist of his hand. His left hand, even though the urge to do the same also came from his right.

Impossible, the doctors always said. The phantom pain should've gone by now.

No matter what they gave him, nothing made it go away. Yano doubted it ever would.

Dana stirred next to him; one arm flopped over and landed just above his head.

"Another dream?" Her voice was heavy with sleep. She always knew when he woke up from one. Some change in his movement only she seemed attuned to.

Carefully, Yanos slid his legs over the side and managed to lift himself out of bed. Naked, he walked stiffly into the ensuite and reached for the light switch. Swallowing a breath, he reached around and used his left arm as he had meant to.

The light stung his eyes, forcing them closed. Squinting through the glare, he turned the tap in the sink, filled a glass, and left the water running as he drank.

By the time he was finished, he could open his eyes fully and stared at his reflection in the mirror. New stubble showed itself along his jaw and cheeks, and his eyes looked a little bloodshot from lack of sleep. They always did, though, so he paid them no mind.

His right arm always drew his gaze, no matter how

much he tried to focus on other features.

The truncated stump ended a good bit above the elbow, the remaining piece of it encased in a brass cage designed to fit into his prosthetic. It looked like a metalwork sculpture.

Yanos hated the fucking thing.

To him, it looked like a parasite had latched itself onto his arm. Horrific as the description sounded, he found it impossible not to think of it in such a way.

Dana appeared in the mirror. She came up behind him, her hair tousled from sleep. Sliding one arm around him, she turned the tap off and rested her other hand on his shoulder.

"You should think about what Peter said," she spoke with her chin resting against his back.

"I know." He hated to admit it. "I just might have to."

"You can't keep this up." She faced him in the mirror. "Teaching isn't as soft as you thought it would be."

Yanos managed a laugh. "No, it's not."

"Speak to Peter in the morning, see what he says." She kissed his stubbly cheek. "Come back to bed when you're ready."

He watched her reflection walk away.

Yanos looked at his stump once more, returned the glass to its place on the shelf, and made his way back to bed.

Dressing in the morning was something between ritual and torture for Yanos. Some days, it was more one— and some days, more the other. Only Dana made any of it tolerable.

In the beginning, he'd had a problem with her helping him. But it became obvious very quickly that fitting his arm was a two-man operation.

Inert, it weighed more than a limb of flesh and bone could, and it rested on a specially made stand when he didn't wear it. Active, he could crush a skull with it or put it through a man's body.

Most of his time in the hospital after the surgery revolved around learning to do neither. It was like learning to walk all over again, only this time, he could do more than cry at his frustration.

Dana rubbed salve where his skin joined the interface plugs, while Yanos finished adjusting his trousers. Each of them had fallen into a rut of routine when it came to this now more-complicated task.

Gently, he ran a hand around his ribs under the stump, feeling for where each of the wire bundles joined the sockets.

"Everything alright?"

"Fine, I think." He nodded, probing for any break in the connections. "No, it's fine."

Her fingers massaged the clear gel delicately around each socket, making each one pivot in place. The sensation made his skin break out in goosebumps as the wires moved in sympathy with the socket, rubbing faintly against his rib bones and under his skin.

It was better than the skin going first raw and then inflamed, and finally infected.

When she finished with the salve, she wheeled the stand over and positioned it so he could lock his stump into the socket provided. As soon as the brass fittings clicked into place, the gears and micro pistons along the length of the arm came to life. Yanos flexed each of the brass-trimmed fingers in turn before opening and closing the hand a few times.

Dana slid a series of slender black cables into their corresponding sockets and the procedure was completed. She helped him into his shirt, minus a right sleeve, then helped him button it and adjust his suspenders over his shoulders.

The end of it came when she forced him to button his tunic alone, while she arranged his ribbons along his left breast. It had taken him months of crushed buttons to finally master the technique of doing his jacket up.

She brushed imaginary specks of dust from his shoulders and straightened his collar a fraction. "Remember to speak to Peter."

He leaned in and kissed her neck. "Don't worry, I will."

The war college campus was always quiet between seven and eight, all but the most ardent students staying in bed until the alarms went. It was a different place from the old days, Yanos often reflected. *A revolution will do that.*

Party posters and bills were tacked and plastered to every available notice board. Lists of various student societies and clubs, many pre-revolution, fought for space where they could.

He passed a couple of students, their dark green uniforms looking freshly pressed as he made his way across the quadrangle. They came up short and saluted crisply, a gesture Yanos was forced to return with the brass-trimmed augmetic.

It whirred as he brought it up and hissed ever so slightly as he lowered it once again to his side.

Passing under the arch leading to the lecture halls and faculty offices, he saw a black town car parked near the entrance to one of the halls. A pair of small flags bearing the party insignia flapped lazily in the morning breeze.

The driver looked towards him, got out of the car a moment later, and went behind to open the passenger door for someone Yanos couldn't make out.

Yanos stopped when he saw who it was, then carried on, changing his course to meet the new arrival. Without thinking, he stuck out his augmetic hand to shake and didn't realise until later how well he'd controlled it.

"Yanni, good to see you again," Buhler said, cracking a grin.

"You too, sir."

Buhler, one of the three party deputy chairmen, shushed him down. "Enough of that *sir* business, it's still just Jurgen to friends."

Buhler. The last time I saw him, he was thirty pounds lighter and close to shitting his brains out from gut rot. Despite the memory, Yanos smiled. *The joys of living in a trench with no clean water.* He had to admit, things were simpler then.

"What brings you here, party business?"

"Something like that, but I was hoping to catch you as well." Buhler took in the old buildings and towers surrounding them. "Suit you well enough?"

"It does."

"Never pegged you for a teacher."

Yanos felt a small spasm in his arm, probably just a small feedback pulse. "Things change."

Buhler seemed to notice the augmetic for the first time since his arrival. "I suppose they do."

Stopping in front of the entrance to the memorial hall, Buhler laid a hand on Yanos' arm. "You should think about your future, after this place."

"These days, I don't think that far ahead, Juri."

"You should. There are places for men like you. God knows we can do with more of the old guard where it counts."

"Didn't realise I was 'old guard.'"

Buhler smiled. "None of us are the boys we once were."

After his morning class, only half full because of the athletic trials held at the same time, Yanos went to find Peter.

Being a creature of habit, Peter would most likely be in his office, pouring over piles of essays. Officers sitting the medical courses had year-round exams due to the new curriculum brought in last year. Peter always looked haggard these days, but when Yanos found him, he looked surprisingly bright for what must have been a hard morning.

"Yanni," he beamed, dropping the paper he was reading and beckoning his friend over. "Thank god." He waved a hand at his desk, buried under mounds of text books and folders. "Come to save me from this invasion."

"I'll do what I can." He looked around the small room for a space to sit.

Peter pointed to a chair, already occupied with more folders. "Just drop that anywhere."

Yanos shifted them to the floor and took the seat, noticing how rickety the thing felt when he put his weight down.

"What can I do for you?" Peter pointed to his arm. "It giving you any trouble? I know a new specialist if you want a referral."

"No, that's not why I'm here."

The penny dropped, and Peter slipped his spectacles from his face.

"Oh, right."

"You mentioned a retreat…is that what it was?"

"Yes."

"Dana…she suggested I should."

Peter smiled sympathetically. "The last time I mentioned it, I got the opposite impression."

Yanos shifted uncomfortably in his chair. "That's one way you could put it," he said weakly. "I'm sorry for that."

"No, no." Peter twirled his glasses. "It's alright…maybe I wasn't as sensitive as I should've been."

An embarrassed pause settled between them, then Yanos swallowed and continued. "Is there still a chance I can pay it a visit?"

"Of course, its intake runs all year."

"When could I leave?"

Peter replaced his glasses, adjusting the wire legs behind his ears with care. "Let me make calls to a few people," he said as he looked at the clock on the wall above the window. "Where will you be around three?"

"The south hall for my theory class."

"Right. Well, I'll find you then and let you know."

The rest of his day passed as it should have. He took his dinner with the students in the dining hall and spoke to those with dissertations due at the end of term. He chatted to the other lecturers, most of whom were his senior by at least twenty years. Old staff officers no longer suitable for command.

Yanos appreciated them where others didn't. They might meander and drone on and on, but their stories always carried a point sometimes lost on the students.

He had more in common with the old buffers than with the students. The students reminded him too much of himself when he was newly minted and turned out. The mud, blood, and shit soon took the shine out of his eyes, along with the arm.

Peter knocked on the door of the emptying lecture hall, falling back against the tide of young men eager to get outside while there was still light. It had turned into a beautiful day after the cloudiness of the morning.

"What did your friends say?"

"No problems, but I didn't expect there to be. You can turn up whenever you want."

Yanos had hoped Peter was going to say something else, but hid it behind an easy smile. "Good, it'll put Dana at ease."

Peter put his hands in his pockets and shuffled his feet

on his way out. "Let me know when you leave."

"How long can you wear it?" Dana arranged some clothes in a small case.

"The doctors said I could wear it to bed, if I wanted." He tapped the knot of fittings making up the elbow. "Just have to be careful about the plugs."

She hadn't looked up from the case when she spoke. Yanos wanted to put an arm on her shoulder, but decided against it.

As hard as it had been for him to adjust, it was harder for her. He'd not been the most generous or patient of people after the surgery. Things were said he could never take back, and he was reconciled to the idea they would always lie between them.

"Alright then."

She finished and closed the case, then held it out to him at arm's length. He took it, their fingers touching for too short a time.

The retreat was an old mansion, once the property of an old landed family dispossessed of their holdings after the revolution.

Gravel crunched under Yanos' shoes as he strolled up the wide drive. A blustery wind tugged at his coat and patches of dark clouds periodically blocked the sun, threatening to spill rain down on him. A couple of old town cars were parked to either side of the main doors, but otherwise, there was no sign of life.

Unsure of what to expect or where to go, he ambled

up to the entrance and touched a finger to the rusting call button.

Half expecting it not to work, Yanos was surprised when the doors opened and a young woman in trousers, shirt, and a faded uniform jacket stepped out. Her dark hair was tied in a tight bun behind her head and she wore no makeup.

"Major."

He stuck out a hand and was surprised at the strength of her grip.

"I'm Doctor Remenova."

"Happy to meet you."

"Are you?" She turned her mouth slightly at the corners. "Everyone says that."

Beyond the door, the first floor opened out into a foyer. Decorated columns had once lined the walls; their absence marked where they had been.

"There are ten patients at the moment."

"And they're all…," he broke off shyly.

"Like you? Yes, Major," she said as they walked up a flight of stairs to a second floor corridor lined with doors on either side. "They've all had similar problems."

"What did Peter say?"

"Nothing we wouldn't expect to hear from someone who suffered a trauma as you have." She stopped in front of one door and opened it.

The room inside was simple, but functional. A single bed and a window with a small balcony. A table and chair and a wash stand with an enamel basin.

"I'll leave you to get settled. The others are downstairs

in the canteen, you can't miss it."

"Yanni?"

Yanos turned and froze for a moment, not recognising the face confronting him.

It was scarred down its left side, and the eye on the same side had been replaced with an intricate substitute. He could see the bronze-coloured ring banding the iris.

"Michal?" Yanos stepped forward and gently embraced his friend in a hug.

"I heard about what happened to you," Michal said. "Didn't think this place was your sort of thing."

"Neither did I." He found his gaze drawn to the artificial eye and the scars marring his friend's face. "I didn't know you'd been hurt…sorry." It felt like a flat platitude on his tongue, but Michal didn't seem to notice.

"We never did stay in touch."

"No…I thought about trying, but I didn't know where to start."

"What are you doing these days?"

"Teaching at the war college."

Michal beamed. "You? Times certainly have changed, haven't they?"

Yanos held up his arm. "For both of us."

The structure of their time revolved around meals. Yanos expected them to sit in a circle and talk about their experiences, but that wasn't how it was going to be.

"Staff are on hand, just in case," Remenova explained. "But otherwise, your stay here is entirely voluntary. You can leave whenever you want."

"Then what's the point?"

"You'll open up among yourselves without any help from us. I've seen it happen."

"Peter never mentioned your methods."

"They're unconventional, but we've met with good results. I can see by the look on your face you have doubts, but trust me. You're all better qualified to help each other than we are."

Yanos took her at her word, deciding to stay for Michal, if nothing else. His friend might do a good job of hiding it, but they'd schooled together for eight years as cadets. He could see when he was being eaten up inside.

Can he see the same in me? he wondered. *Can all of them?*

Trying and failing to read one of the books he'd brought with him, Yanos let it drop onto his chest and stared up at the ceiling. He'd stripped his jacket and shirt off, surprising himself with the ease with which he disconnected the arm.

Dana might have appreciated it.

A knock came from the other side of his door and it opened a moment later.

Michal put one foot in and stopped. "Oh, sorry. Are you busy?"

"No, Michal, come in."

Gingerly, Michal did, and slid the chair away from the table to the foot of the bed.

"Can't sleep?" Yanos asked.

"No. Not very good at it anymore."

"Hm," Yanos breathed. "What, em…what happened to you?"

"Show you mine if you show me yours?" Michal offered a smile that didn't lighten the mood. "I was hoping you would ask."

"None of the others opened up yet?"

"Did she explain what they do here?"

"Yes, she told me exactly what goes on here."

"What do you think?"

"I've heard stranger theories about making people better."

Michal's eye glinted in the light of the wall lamps. "You think we can ever be better?"

Yanos sat up and put his feet on the floor one by one. "I think if we don't try, we'll never know."

Michal lifted himself out of the chair. He looked at the caged stump of Yanos' arm. "Can you do it yourself?"

"It's easier with help," he admitted.

Michal looked pensive, unsure if helping Yanos would hurt him.

"You don't have to."

"No, it's okay."

For a long time, Michal stared at the brass arm on the table. His eyes traced the pattern of the coils and gears before he picked it up, cradling it against his chest to better take the weight.

Yanos bent his knees, inserted the stump, and twisted. There was an audible clack as mechanisms locked into place. The arm came partially to life, the fingers waggling slowly.

"What now?" Michal still held the arm, afraid to let go

in case it fell.

"The plugs." Yanos held one up to show him. "I'll do the front, if you can manage the back?"

"It's okay to let it hang?"

Yanos nodded and slotted the first plug into a socket beneath his chest. Twisting it sent a faint pulse through the arm. Copying the action, Michal matched each plug to its entry point.

Yanos felt Michal's fingers brush against the slightly raw skin surrounding the sockets. They were rough and calloused, so unlike Dana's, but more comforting in their own way. Nothing except long absence lay between them, but it was a gap that could be bridged.

Michal twisted the last plug, locking it into place. He stepped back as Yanos turned, but for a second, they were face to face. Their bodies almost touched for the briefest of moments, allowing something imperceptible to pass between them.

They both felt it; the sensation was not alien, merely old from lack of association.

Outside, the sky was clear. Seeing by the light of the moon, they traipsed across the grounds surrounding the mansion, heading in the direction of a small copse of trees. Michal carried a bottle of cooking brandy appropriated from the kitchens, the contents sloshing in time with the sway of his hands.

"I don't really remember what happened," he began. "When I try to, I only see a flash of light, like a star shell going off in my hand, and then nothing."

Yanos thought him the more fortunate for it. His own memories were a non-sequitur jumble of moments intercutting on each other. His dreams were more coherent, but this only brought the moments closer to a linear narrative, sharpening them in the process.

"This place almost reminds me of school," Michal continued, changing subjects in the space of a few steps. "The playing fields."

"I was thinking that just now."

"Remember the state we all got into when we found the key to Mr. Stefl's bottom drawer?" Michal unscrewed the cap and splashed some of the brandy down his throat.

Yanos smiled and accepted Michal's offer of the bottle. "I remember the running track covered in puke, but not much else."

"Ha, they caned our backsides raw."

"I'd almost forgotten that bit." Of course, that wasn't true. The night after might have happened yesterday to Yanos, but he wasn't sure enough in himself to say it. Not yet.

Under the thin canopy of the copse, there was just enough moonlight to see by. They were both tipsy enough by the time they reached it for what light there was to be of no use whatsoever.

"Yanni?" Michal held onto a tree as though it and not he was going to fall.

"Hmm?"

"What's that?"

Yanos stopped by his friend's side, looking in the same

direction. It took him a moment to see the solid shape in the middle of the trees through his watery eyes.

"Summer house, maybe?"

Michal let go of the tree and stumbled forward, his feet catching on roots as he went.

It was a summer house, or something like one. The glass in the windows was long since gone and the door hung askew on its only good hinge. Thick dust covered the wooden floor, and something small scurried from its hiding place when they went inside.

To their surprise, two rickety chairs were upended against the wall. Neither one looked like it could take much weight, but they were drunk enough to risk it.

Michal held his arms out as though he was going to start flapping like a bird. His chair creaked, buckled slightly, and settled as he leaned back.

Yanos simply sat, causing some part of the chair to crack with a dull snap, though nothing visible broke away. Realising he still held the bottle, he took a swig of the horrible brandy and held it out to Michal.

"I never thanked you," Yanos said.

"For what?"

"Letting me in…gods, we were both so young."

"Out of our depth."

"I was so drawn to you."

"I know…and I was to you." Michal bit his lip. "I still am." He leaned forward, hands and bottle dangling off his knees. Gently, he slipped his hand around the augmetic limb.

Yanos tried to pull away for a moment, but gave in

and returned the gesture, running his hand over Michal's scarred face. He brushed the skin around his eye with a forefinger, the glint of metal around the iris barely visible in the darkness.

"Look at us both, Mica..."

"Look at what they made us."

Yanos left after one day more, passing the time in Michal's company and talking about nothing. He never saw him alive again after that time, and he never told his wife about what passed between them.

Dana met him on the steps of their campus house when he got back. It was late, but neither he nor she was tired.

"How was it?" She stood hugging herself against the cold.

She started when he took her wrist in the cold metal of his augmetic. The grip was so soft it could almost have come from a flesh and blood hand.

He kissed her once and held her. "Can we talk in the morning?" he asked.

For the first time in a long time, he did not dream that night. He accepted what he was, having learned to let go of who he had been before. It was Michal's gift to him, though he would only realise it later when it was too late to thank him.

Deviant

"Cancer, really?" Daye slumped, deflated with a breath. "You're sure?"

"I'll run a second battery of tests, but I don't think they'll show anything different." Wood, a doctor Daye more or less trusted, linked his hands together on the dull chrome of his desk. "It's not as bad as it sounds." He tried a smile on and thought the better of it. "We caught it early."

Daye wasn't really paying attention, his eyes flitting left and right. They were turning thoughts around and around in his head. "But I was gene coded at birth."

Wood nodded. "You probably picked something up from the de-con suites." No one liked to think they weren't one hundred percent efficient. "It's rare, but it's not unheard of."

"When did someone last die of cancer?"

"I'd have to check, but not since the middle of the last century, I think."

Daye pursed his lips, opened and closed his mouth, and straightened a bit in his chair. "Alright, so what happens now?"

"I'll sign you off and get you into the clinic today." Wood consulted a tablet. It faded into view in his hand, already compiled by the station's cloud server. "You'll be off for about three or four days. I'll put you into an induced coma for the re-code and immuno graft." He clicked his tongue. "There are side effects for adults."

"Like what?"

"Nausea and stomach and muscle cramps. Your body will be full of semi-toxic antibodies for a day before it adjusts."

"Fucking great."

"You're in the best place for it." Wood did smile this time. "The station's fully equipped."

Daye felt as though he should be reassured, but couldn't muster much in the way of the feeling. He was always careful. It felt like it was his own fault, and he wanted Wood to say so. He could handle that more than he could the idea it was down to random bad luck.

The worst part was he couldn't think of when he'd been careless enough for it to have happened.

"Okay." It was only a formality to agree, but it still felt right to say it. At least it provided some measure of control.

Pain brought him slowly up, his mind clawing its way out from under a fog of induced stillness.

Daye wasn't waking so much as he was regaining consciousness. Dimly, the difference floated around in the back of his mind. A thought freed by tiredness.

Clean white light forced his eyes closed as soon as he opened them. How long had he been asleep? The burning numbness in his back suggested longer that three or four days. He wasn't sure if he could move his legs.

Slowly and one at a time, he opened his eyes, blinking away tears before he was able to focus. Thankfully, the suite's automated systems looked to have kept removing his piss and shit while he'd been under. That was something to be grateful for.

Pressing his hands flat on the bed, he pushed himself up. Halfway to sitting, his arms started trembling. Wavering and ready to fall back, he slid his numb buttocks along to lever himself forward.

"Fuck." It came out as a hoarse croak, stealing what little moisture was left in his throat and mouth.

Sweat beaded on his forehead, running and trickling its way into his eyes, He didn't risk raising a hand to wipe it away. Someone should know he was awake, so why wasn't anyone here already?

Parking the thought, Daye looked down at his legs. They were pale and looked too thin, and he wasn't sure if he could use them. They jerked when he tried to shift or else remained more or less still, like deadweights.

Feeling able to hold himself up without his hands, he reached down and flicked a finger against the flesh of his thigh. It stung, which meant the nerves were okay. The muscles just hadn't been used. He'd been under a while.

More than four days. He didn't want to think about exactly how long. Cramps pulled his abdomen in on itself, squeezing his stomach and pushing it upwards.

Daye just managed to crane his neck over the edge of the bed, but the effort of dry heaving dragged him all the way over. He landed hard with a wet-sounding thwack, like meat hitting an abattoir floor. The air was knocked out of his lungs.

Fighting for breath, he pressed his cheek against the floor tiles. They were cool and more welcoming than the bed had been.

He remembered where a pair of supports was stored in a locker, Wood's habit of hanging onto surplus equipment no longer seeming quite so eccentric.

Daye crawled until he was able to lift himself up on the support rail running the length of the outside corridor. Fixed to the wall or not, he was sure it was going to break off under his weight. He found his arms in little better shape than his legs, but they were a little better all the same.

Every step caused his stomach to lurch, and his feet felt ready to twist under him in their deadness.

By the time he reached the locker, he was soaked in sweat. He breathed in big gulps, burning his already-dry throat to sandpaper. His head was swimming, but he managed to hold back another urge to puke.

The supports were an old model, but still functional. The hardest part was getting them on. They didn't open all the way, like the newer ones did, only splitting husk-like as far as the ankle, where they formed boot-like covers for his feet.

Fastening them around his waist, Daye slipped his sodden shirt off and replaced it with a black one that he'd found hanging in the locker. A little baggy, maybe, but it was clean and felt soft against his clammy skin.

His fingers fumbled with the small buttons set flush where the supports gripped his hips. After a few failed jabs, he managed it and they sealed shut, closing along the seam silently. Tightening around his thighs and calf muscles, they locked and took his weight.

It fucking hurt; the grip was unrelenting. At least he could walk, however uncomfortable it might be. He reckoned he could probably manage a run, if he needed to, and he was thinking it might come to that.

No one passed him in the corridor. Even if the suite's monitoring system had failed, there were cameras implanted every five meters in the walls. No one coming to help meant no one was responding to an alert from the AI.

The station had a crew of twenty-five, standard for one of its size. There were a handful of possible situations he could think of that would clear the decks, but even if one of those were the case, there still should have been some sign of life.

That was it. The silence was fit to deafen him. It was an absence of movement or life.

Awkwardly, Daye took his first step. Nano-fiber bundles creaked from lack of use, but soon quieted as he clumped his way down the rest of the corridor.

The main access way was dark in places, the first real sign that something was seriously wrong.

A light blinked on a still-active console. Daye crossed to it and pressed his thumb to the scanner. There was a short delay before it chirped and came to life. The display was partly incomplete, fading to dark in places and flickering with static tracking.

His code was still good, the system having read his ident tag from his haptic frame. He needed a layout of the station, but had to bypass several defunct systems to access the core memory. At least the secondary AI looked to be intact, but it would only come online if the primary was down.

Something banged above his head and the noise reverberated through the deck plate.

"Fuck." He couldn't manage to jump in fear, but rocked back as the support fought to keep him upright.

Light from the console shaded into blue, pulling his attention back. Parts of the station quickly shifted to red or black in a few places.

"Shit."

The station had shifted on its axis, drifting towards Sholant, the gas giant it orbited. The drift wasn't much, but eventually it would reach a point of no return and tumble into the storm-tossed atmosphere.

From here, it was impossible for Daye to access any of the still-functioning systems. Medical and most of the hardware below the neck required the primary AI for operations.

Plotting the best possible route to the nest, the station's main control hub, he uploaded it to his frame. A way marker flashed up, shaped like a hollow triangle made from yellow light.

Sounds seemed to stalk Daye as he made his way along the route. Sometimes far away and other times much closer, the acoustics of the station made their distance hard to judge.

He thought that maybe it could be the result of internal damage. Without a diagnostic and with so many sections dark, it made sense, but he had no way of being sure.

Forty-five minutes, and still no people; the sounds

might be survivors.

Passage between the decks didn't look impossible, so he reasoned that he should've met someone. The noises were being caused by something else.

He stamped the thought flat before it could fully form.

It was like he'd gone to sleep in one place and woken up in another. The station was both familiar and unfamiliar at the same time, but robbed of its inhabitants, it could've been anywhere. Daye found himself checking his haptic frame more often, interfacing wherever he could just to make sure he was in the right place.

A few hundred meters short of the incubation ring, the frame refused to connect. He was beyond the reach of the server. Everything forward of this point was a dead zone.

With luck, he'd be able to find a functioning console and raise someone when he got there.

Beyond the hatch, the ring looked more or less intact, only the door was partially ripped from its combing. It was buckled and still hanging limply, forced outwards from the inside.

His feet crunched pieces of broken glass as he walked inside. Like the door, the variant's incubation tanks were shattered from the inside. Finding the most-intact terminal, he activated it manually and found the active scan system still operational.

Before he could sweep the station, Daye stopped.

A displacement in the air; not something he was

consciously aware of. The kind of feeling when you know someone's close at hand, almost right behind you. A weight pressing against your back without needing to touch.

A shiver went up his spine. He didn't want to turn, but couldn't stop himself.

Whatever it was now, it had been a variant. That much was clear to Daye.

The head was still more or less human-shaped, but the resemblance started and ended there. Its legs were formed into reverse-jointed limbs more like hands, of which there were eight. Its skin was mottled and roughened to the texture of cracked leather.

A nest of pupil-black eyes of different sizes formed a ring around its head, with two larger ones like dinner plates where most of its face should have been. It didn't crawl, but scuttled forward like a spider with too long a body.

Daye took a couple of steps, the supports refusing to translate the movement into a dead run, before it tackled him. Sprawling across Daye, it raised one of its legs and brought it down.

Daye noticed the hand at the end of it was almost human, the palm pinkish like his own and the fingers more or less the right shape. He couldn't decide if that was the most horrifying thing. He jerked his head aside and grabbed the next one it tried to kill him with, and the one after that, but he couldn't beat its advantage in limbs.

The fingers flexed all too humanlike, clawing for his face as it pushed down. Its eyes were depthless, black pools swallowing what light there was.

Fingertips brushed against his cheek and Daye wanted

to scream. He felt it jerk crazily as the front of its head broke open, spilling ichor down Daye's neck and face.

It fell in a dead weight.

Gagging on the taste of its blood, he started to move it, but another set of hands reached down to help him.

"Daye?" Alena rolled the once-variant off and stared at him. "Where the fuck did you come from?"

He was happy to see Alena. She wasn't his favorite person. There was no real reason for it, they just hadn't clicked.

"What's going on?"

Alena let her mouth hang open a little. "Have you been under a rock or something?"

"More or less." He explained his diagnosis and waking up in the medical suite.

"Shit, you've no idea."

"Alena, what the fuck is happening." He jabbed a finger at the body. The variant was curling up on itself, folding like a pinned insect. "What happened to it?"

It had started not long after they put Daye under, though it was too late by the time anyone noticed the problem. Maybe it was the same whatever that Daye had picked up—it was impossible to say. It escaped de-con and went from there.

Once inside the genetic cascade and once combined with the raw material inside, it slipped into the incubation ring and compromised the variants.

"They went rampant." Alena paused for a moment to

let it sink in.

Rampancy. When variants became deviants. Daye could count the number of times it had happened on one hand and still have fingers left over. Each instance was decades apart.

He was able to work out he'd been out of surgery a day when everything hit the fan. Once it flooded the tanks, there was nothing to be done. Normal procedure was to dump the litter and move on. Only no one counted on the changes it would cause in them.

"Alena, where is everyone?"

"As far as I know, they're dead."

"No one got to the boats?"

"By the time we gave up on lock-down, it was too late." She rubbed her face, pressing the heels of her palms hard against her eyes. "The last time I saw someone was a day ago."

Four days then. Only the fact of being asleep had kept Daye alive.

"Can the boats still launch?"

Alena shrugged. "The nest is a no-go. Upper levels are crawling with them."

"Manual?"

"The problem is getting close to the boats." She brought up the launch ports on the console. "They know the station. We fed them all the information," she said, swiping her hands across the board. The image switched to highlight the launch ports. "They're waiting for someone to try."

Staying on the station wasn't an option. If the deviants

didn't do for them, the decaying orbit would.

The nest. It was all he could think. From primary command, it would be possible to look at more options. Assuming it was possible to reach it.

One of Alena's annoying habits was her ability to read him. "We'd never make it."

"We've got to get off the station."

"We're off the net. Someone'll be heading our way."

"Without much clue about what they're walking into." A thought struck him. "You know the orbit's decaying?"

"No."

He showed her. It was worse than before, but there was still time before the hull temp started rising noticeably.

"Shit, I never thought to check."

Understandable; it wasn't at the point where it could be felt.

"There might be a way to get past them."

"I'm open to ideas."

She wasn't going to like it any more than he did.

If Daye was honest with himself, it was hard to trust her. The look she gave him told him she probably felt the same way. It wasn't so much bad blood as a lack of understanding between them. He couldn't trust her not to ditch him, and he couldn't say he wouldn't understand if she did.

He decided he'd at least try and be the bigger man and make the effort. All they had was each other.

Getting to the nest meant going through the neck, a spire-work of companionways cutting the station in half.

Airlocks lined the central access at various intervals—a blowout measure in case of disaster. It allowed half of the station to isolate itself from the other.

Through the armored glass window, the neck was dark, save for the intermittent strobe pulse of red emergency lights. He caught a spatter of dark smears along part of the wall on the other side.

Alena popped the manual release, the pneumatic handle easing out of its cavity.

"There are definitely less of them on this side," she said as she opened the grip, which splayed out into something like the business end of a shovel for better leverage.

She'd been jumpy on the way here, looking back over her shoulder once or twice. Daye put it down to what they were about to do, but had also developed a feeling that something was following close behind. Clangs and bangs echoed behind them, as if something was moving through the shafts lacing the station like arteries.

That nothing emerged to rip them apart didn't make the feeling go away.

The neck presented a good place for the deviants to gather, the data loaded into them and their animal instincts would tell them so. Those same instincts could be used against them.

Once the door was open, there was no going back. Alena handed him the weld caster she'd used to kill the deviant back in the ring.

"Don't piss it away." She pumped the handle once, twice, three times. The door slid open painfully slowly until it was wide enough to squeeze through.

She went first and Daye followed, having to twist his body because of his leg supports.

Once they were both on the other side, she took off at a dead run. He'd tweaked the supports with her help, so he was at least capable of a fast walk and started off after her.

The red strobe pulsed, each flash freezing Alena for a second. She was a gradually diminishing figure, moving out of synch with the echo of her footsteps. Daye pounded along the corridor, careful to make as much noise as possible.

He shot the first deviant as it came at him from the roof, moving faster than he could credit. Its chest blew open under the impact of the micro-thin steel shaft, sending it tumbling over his head behind him.

Daye didn't stop. He could hear them stirring in the connecting corridors, a constant susurrus as they made their way towards him.

He guessed he was maybe a quarter of the way down the passage. It was probably less. His legs ached, and sweat glued his shirt to his chest and back. Without the supports, he'd have toppled over by now.

Chancing a glance over his shoulder, which he regretted thanks to the strobe suggesting flitters of movement, he fired blindly back down the way he'd come.

A wet popping sound and a dissonant series of screeches told him he'd hit something. They must be tightly packed, pushing over each other in their rush to get to him.

Fuck being the better man if this was what it got you.

A twisted shadow lumbered towards him, revealed by the strobe as a misshapen thing leaping for Daye. The second's worth of light left disconnected pieces burned across his vision. What might have been hands fused to hooked blades and bulbous eyes with crazed facets.

Daye depressed the trigger and pissed away too much, exactly as Alena had told him not to. Ichor and body parts splashed and bounced into him, and something heavy clunked onto the deck near his feet.

Fire stabbed into his back, ripping fabric and skin as he wrenched himself out of its reach. It only helped whatever was clawing at him dig its claws in deeper.

Quick and steady, he changed out the magazine and fired single shots whether he had a clear target or not. The confines of the corridor and the way they were clambering over each other were probably the only reasons he wasn't dead yet.

C'mon, fucker. He knew the flimsiest part of all this was on Alena's end. Assuming she'd even made it to the other side.

She could also have just popped the door and carried on without him. Daye couldn't put it past her, because he knew he'd likely do the same or at least think about it.

A brittle-looking hand clamped around his ankle and yanked back hard. Daye almost went down, but threw his free leg out in front to steady himself. Again he squeezed the trigger and held it, spraying in a blind arc behind and around him.

The strobe revealed only an amorphous mass of distended limbs, all writhing and clawing their way over each other. The hand grabbing his ankle snapped like dry wood and he dragged it along with him.

Pressed in or not, they were starting to push hard against each other. The whole mass would pop forward like a champagne cork and the tide would swamp him. It was only a question of whether he could turn the caster on himself in time.

Daye caught the sound of whistling. Air started to gust down the corridor in the direction he'd come from. The first airlock was open.

Maybe it was the growing lack of air going to his head in combination with malnutrition and adrenaline; later, he would never be sure or have time to care either way. He expended a bolt and blew the knee lock from his supports. The other one followed. He broke into a shambling run and shrugged the remains of the apparatus free.

Acid burned his muscles and his head swam worse than before as the wind picked up. It tugged at him and blew itself into a gale as more locks opened. A deviant screeched through the air, its body pivoting end over end in relation to the roof. One hand with too many fingers raked across his face as it clawed for something to stop itself.

The door appeared in the strobe moment, split along its middle. Unopened, he would've suffocated a while ago.

The last meter took his legs out from under him and Daye pushed the caster out in front as he crawled.

Alena braced herself in the gap, one hand reaching out towards him. She grabbed the business end of the caster instead of him and pulled.

Daye was never sure if she'd meant to do it on

purpose. In the moment she took hold of it, his own grip was loose, and it all but slipped from his hand.

"No," his voice was snatched away by the rushing wind.

It sounded like she was saying something. It sounded like 'Fucking bastard,' but it could've been to urge him on rather than to let go. He hauled himself towards her, nearly over-balancing her as he pulled against her.

Once through the door, she slammed the release back up, closing and sealing everything out. The metal grew cold very fast, creaking as it contracted against the void.

The wall near where Daye sprawled was a mess of wires and leads, mostly ripped out and rigged together.

Alena rolled him over. "Jesus."

His vision was tinged red, meaning a burst blood vessel or two. The skin of his right cheek felt tight where he'd been clawed.

"I'm fine," he managed.

She propped him up against her as they made their way towards the nest. Daye thought she seemed twitchier than before. Possibly the result of not seeing any deviants on this side of the neck, though the feeling they'd had earlier hadn't gone away.

They'd passed a body a few meters beyond the door; a woman Daye had quite liked. He'd needed to look twice before he was sure it was her.

A broken rail, one end matted with what might have been blood, finally took the place of Alena's shoulder. She kept pace beside him, caster held ready at the waist. Creaks and clatters followed them, always behind them and around a corner.

"It's the structure taking the loss in pressure," Daye said, trying to make himself believe it. "On manual, the door seal won't be perfect."

She nodded. "How do you feel?"

"Better." It was a relative term. His eyes felt blistered, a feeling he'd never thought they were capable of experiencing. His head throbbed dully, but his legs no longer shook so much from lack of use.

"Something's following us," she whispered.

Daye knew it, but didn't want to draw the connection with that first sound he'd heard after leaving medical. It meant that it was following him. Alena was just unlucky enough to be with him.

"Nothing can cross the neck now."

Neither of them felt the need to contemplate that it might have crossed ahead of them.

Not much further now, if his guess was right. There had to be something still working in the nest.

Something buckled; a panel in the roof, perhaps. The sound like a gunshot made them both jump, though they did their best to control it.

Damage in the nest looked near total. While some of the consoles still blinked, Daye wasn't hopeful any of them would be of any use.

There were no bodies, but there was enough dried blood to suggest several people died here.

Alena laid the caster down on one of the consoles and

brought it to life. Daye went to her side and peered at the display. Only half the emergency lights were functioning, and the gloom was like a shroud over everything.

"Haptic's are still fucked." She operated it manually, her fingers a little clumsy from lack of practice on the keys.

This part of the station was in bad shape, and none of the nest's mainframe links were active. Alena had to access the diagrams from the secondary AI. It wasn't ideal, but it granted them a fuller picture than they'd enjoyed so far.

One bank of lifeboats two levels down was still active, able to launch once occupied.

"What's that?" He traced the tracking interference breaking up the picture. Only it couldn't be that, because it was too regular.

"Motion sensors. As fried as the station is, the AI's still at least partially hooked into the monitor feeds…could be a fault."

Neither of them believed it was.

"How many do you think?"

"A lot."

Fuck.

Through the fog of his pounding head, Daye almost missed it. A wet, animal breathing, air being inhaled and exhaled through a nose or mouth soaked in mucus. Leaning on the pole, he turned slowly and looked into the shadows blanketing parts of the nest.

Darker against the darkness where it stood, still and quiet save for the tremor of its breathing. Daye got an impression of a tumorous head and a glint of something like a mantis arm. It couldn't be that tall or that thin, but it was, and it didn't seem possible something so big had crept in without a sound, though it had.

Its other arm might've been more human; a floppy, truncated thing, like a child's hand.

Alena ran, dragging the caster from its resting place. He tried and failed to gather enough energy to hate her for it or say something.

It stepped forward without a sound.

For a moment, its warped face came into the half-light, and he saw into what could've been its only eye. The color of a green sea, he saw intelligence and understanding in it. No pain and no anger, no animal instinct, just something clear and lucid.

Daye felt tears trickle down his face as it looked at him before its face passed back into shadow. Its breath disturbed his hair as it neared, oddly sweet-smelling and sickly, like something rotten.

Its head came into the light for a final time and he swore it was smiling at him, until the part that was really its mouth opened on the wrong side of its face.

Mirrors and Shadows

Sharna Rae was drunk. She was drunk often these days, not that she thought about it much. What occupied her thoughts was how she'd ended up in her current state of affairs.

Sharna was a teratologist, not in itself an unusual profession, but one which could land a person in trouble if they were indiscreet. Sharna had been indiscreet.

In the beginning, her indiscretions were small. Lifting the odd book from the university library. Some supplies from the laboratories and specimen rooms.

The end of the whole affair had come the day after she'd entered the black archive.

Nothing really bad had come of it. No monsters or daemons and such were walking the streets of the city. She'd taken nothing, only glanced inside, but rules are rules and her dismissal hearing had been a formality.

"Another, Sharna?" Bailey asked.

She stared at him, trying to focus through the fog of alcohol stewing her brain.

"Why not?" she said and dug into her pockets, managing to scatter coins across the bar top when it felt like she had enough in her hand.

Bailey gave her a dubious look, perhaps regretting the question. Nevertheless, he picked up enough to cover the cost and went to pour her a pint. He returned with it and held the glass an inch or so from the scuffed and battered counter where she sat.

"I think this is your last one."

"Not a problem," she said, swaying slightly on her stool.

He hesitated a moment longer and finally laid it down.

Bailey led her gently, one hand gripping her bicep as he tried to direct her towards the door. He opened it and let her slip free over the threshold, his responsibility ending once she was outside.

"Night, Bailey!" she called back.

The door closed and she was alone in the street.

Sharna couldn't understand if her feet were trying to overtake her body, or if her body was somehow overtaking her feet.

There's a monologue in there, somewhere, she thought. *The Nature of Inebriated Perambulation in Homo Sapiens.* She snorted, putting a hand to her mouth as it grew into a giggle.

She lurched down the street, turned sharply into a side alley and as the laugh turned into a bout of vomiting.

She awoke tangled up in her covers and still fully dressed.

Her dry mouth tasted sour and fur-lined, gummed up at the corners with a mix of sour drink and acidy spit. It didn't seem like she'd soiled herself this time. That was something, at least.

A lingering wash of drink was sloshing around in her head, a growing throb gripping the front of her skull. As hangovers went, it wasn't as bad as some.

When she felt brave enough to open her eyes, Sharna saw she was very clearly not alone in her room.

At first, she said and did nothing, simply stared at him where he sat with his legs crossed in one of the better chairs she still owned.

"You look like shit," he said. "Although better than I expected, given how much you put away last night."

His accent marked him out as well-to-do. As fear cleared her head, Sharna saw this was supported by his clothes. Well-heeled leather boots and black trousers. A crisp-looking shirt and a black cloak, trimmed in fine red fur. A mop of dark hair fell across his forehead and curled to a stop just above his shoulders. His face was sharp, smooth-skinned, and pale.

Sharna mouthed *I* over and over again without actually finding her voice.

"I was hoping you might manage something more original," he said, reading the movement of her lips.

He stood and reached into the folds of his cloak. Sharna drew back, pulling the covers up to her chin for whatever protection they might offer. She flinched as something landed on the bed.

Leaning over after a few moments, she saw a small silver coin lying face up. The engraved face of an old man stared back at her.

Though she'd never seen the man—centuries dead, no one living had—Sharna knew who he was.

"Now then, perhaps you'd best splash some water on your face, don't you think?"

He gave his name as Elles, and he led Sharna to a square several streets away from the Fleet Gate. An unremarkable coach waited and Elles held the door for her to climb in. Once they were inside, he drew the shutters on all the windows so the only light came in from a small slit in the roof.

Hangover notwithstanding, Sharna had questions shuffling around the back of her throat, but kept her tongue firmly behind her teeth. Elles respected her silence and closed his eyes as the coach started moving, though it was clear from his posture he wasn't asleep.

Time stopped running and soon, she had no idea where they were going. Initially, she'd tried to follow the number of turns they took, but after missing one and then several more in quick succession, she'd lost track.

If he wanted to kill me, I suppose he would've by now.

The reassurance of the thought vanished a moment later, because legend said the men and women who carried the silver coin were in the habit of taking their time when it came to killing. At least if the inclination took them.

Sharna coughed and bit back bile. Her stomach roiled and growled and she felt the urge to go to the privy, but said nothing.

Elles opened his eyes moments before the coach stopped, offering what he probably thought was a disarming smile. The effect was lost on Sharna, but she smiled weakly back because she couldn't think of anything else to do. He opened the door, stepped out, and waited for her to follow.

They were in front of a small, elegant arch. Looking around, Sharna saw nothing but high walls and roof tops sticking up above them. Overhead, the sun was past its highest point.

"He's waiting," Elles said.

"Right."

He walked in front of her through the arch, which led into a small courtyard. A plain-looking door at the far wall was the only other portal she could see.

If it was a house, Sharna thought, it was the strangest one she'd seen.

Maybe I expected gargoyles and a fountain?

There were no windows. She knew the tax was up, but didn't think someone would go to such extreme lengths to avoid paying it.

Elles reached the door and opened it, waiting until she was inside before closing it and moving in front of her again. Gas jets burned along the wall, which was lined with mirrors of varying sizes.

Snatching glances at herself, Sharna did her best to adjust her hair, for all the difference it made. Her skin looked unhealthy and damp from a slight sheen of sweat. She couldn't convince herself she didn't reek of drink.

They came to another door underneath two wings of a sweeping staircase. Elles laid a hand on the knob and paused, facing Sharna without the smile from before.

"Don't interrupt him," he advised gently. "He hates it."

Then she was on her own, stepping through as the door was shut and bolted behind her.

The room she found herself in was lit in an odd way. The gas jets arranged with an assortment of mirrors to throw wide cones of light around the centre. The corners and edges of the room were bathed in deep shadow as a result, a gloom that was almost impenetrable.

Aside from a small table and chair, the room looked otherwise bare of decoration.

"Please, Ms. Rae," said a voice from the shadows. "Take a seat."

Sharna didn't jump, but her stomach lurched and she felt her knees tremble. Slowly, she sat.

"You know who I am?"

She felt it was what she should say, even though it was obvious the speaker did.

"You know who I am?"

He wants you to say it.

"You're Nemo."

"Very good."

Sharna heard the smile in his gravelly voice.

"What else?"

"People say you run everything criminal in the city." Sharna swallowed. "That you're an agent of the inquisition and that you're older than most would believe."

"Yes."

Sharna didn't know if he was answering her question or complimenting her on her knowledge of him. "Why am I here?"

"Not yet, Ms. Rae." The floorboards creaked in the dark. "Indulge my game.

"You are Sharna Rae. Once a senior member of the

university faculty," Nemo paused as though reading from a page. "The faculty of esoteric biology and chymeric research…quite a department in its heyday. Teratology was your chosen field."

He enjoys this; I can hear it in his voice.

"Dismissed for academic misconduct." The boards creaked again. "Or breaching the black archive, I believe it's called. Since then, you've become something of a professional drinker."

His voice lacked judgement.

"All of which begs the question," Sharna hesitated. "If I may? Why am I here?" A wheezy laugh came from somewhere behind her, and she fought the urge to turn.

"I could say I admire audacity, which in fact I do…but the truth is your circumstances and my requirements fit neatly into a possible partnership of convenience."

"I should feel flattered, I suppose."

"No one is ever flattered by my attentions," Nemo mused. "No, fear is the chief emotion felt by those who sit where you do."

The gas jets dimmed until they started flickering, burning so low as to plunge the room into semi-darkness. Nemo stepped forward, but in the bad light, his face was only a smeared suggestion of features. He could've been anyone.

"You're using a shadow weaver," Sharna said. She recognised the manipulation of light and darkness. It was an elementary, but effective ward.

"Follow me."

A door hidden in the wall popped loudly, the open

way through it darker still than the darkness shrouding the room. Nemo stepped through and vanished, Sharna trailing hurriedly in his wake.

He led her to a room lit in the same way as the first, only here, the light was manipulated into a circle. It focused in the middle of the floor.

Nemo was concealed in the shadows before Sharna made it through. In the space made by the light were piled four oblong objects. They looked something like beetle shells and appeared to glisten wetly.

It took a moment for Sharna to recognise them. The illuminations in the books at the university didn't do them justice.

"Where did you get these?"

"We both know the answer to that question, Ms. Rae."

"But no one goes to the Veiled Lands."

"And no one who does, comes back," Nemo finished the proverb.

"I've never seen anything like this," explained Sharna. "What I know about the Unkind comes from books and children's stories."

"About what I expected, but it's not an impediment."

Sharna reached out and ran her hand over the nearest object without actually touching it. "Nocturalka," she said. "Incubators."

"Entirely empty of the material they need to work," said Nemo. "I was hoping you might be able to remedy that situation."

Sharna faced the shadows and then looked down at

the specimens. "This is beyond me."

Nemo's answer seemed to come from directly behind her.

"But I think you would enjoy the chance to try."

Elles brought Sharna everything she asked for, and she didn't want to be told the details of how he managed it. She imagined Nemo's network being jerked into life and passing its acquired items back along the chain. Like ants bringing food to their hive.

In a matter of days, her workspace was strewn with books, papers, and an ever-growing assortment of equipment. Quite a lot of it was marked with the university seal.

Developing a routine, Sharna would wake before sunrise to find Elles waiting for her outside her rooms. After the journey to the house, he would disappear with one of the lists she compiled after each day. Lists of new equipment. Books, research papers, and any number of artefacts she thought might give her a new angle.

Even with a lab and a full staff, I could spend my life battering my head against these things and get no further.

She stopped drinking, but her frustration at the lack of any progress sorely tempted her to have a taste. The grinding clarity of a hangover might be just the thing she needed, but she decided against it whenever she actually came close to the door of an inn.

Nemo hadn't forbidden her to drink, but she didn't want to explore the limits of his patience.

Sharna surveyed the food she'd bought from one of

the stalls near the catacomb walk, gnawing at her bottom lip. Nemo's patience would be pushed beyond its limit if she failed.

Pushing her food away, she stalked back to her rooms in a foul mood.

Elles floated around the edge of the room, darting in and out of the shadows as he wanted. Sharna buried her head in a book, recently liberated from a seller on the black moss road. The more she read, the more she realised not just her own ignorance, but that of every author she'd read at university.

"If you have nothing else you need today, Ms. Rae," Elles began, "may I take my leave of you?"

"Somewhere you need to be?"

"Not really, I just don't see the point of me being here if you've nothing for me…unless you enjoy my company?"

Sharna stopped herself from saying something she'd regret. Not that she imagined Nemo would be upset if she offended one of his employees.

"Actually, Elles," she said as she closed the book and faced him. "I do need you to do something for me."

"What do you need?"

"It's not a what…unless you're a particularly prejudiced person." She tore a scrap from a parchment covered in her notes. "I don't even know if he's still alive…the last pogrom was pretty bad."

Realisation dawned on Elles' face. "I can assure you if he did, I will find him."

Sharna handed him the note. "I imagine with your

dandyish nature, you could pass around in their circles without much effort."

"Just another of my many talents."

Karras Andini said he was seven hundred and more years old, although he didn't look a day over thirty-one. He claimed to have been a child and still human when the first pogrom had swept through the city.

Sharna wasn't as surprised to see him as she'd expected to be. The Nightkin had a habit of surviving the periodic pogroms that flared up in the city.

It took Elles less than a day to locate him, and little more than an hour of chatting to persuade him to pay Sharna a visit.

"Haven't seen much of you since they tossed you out of uni," he offered by way of greeting.

They were alone in the room Nemo had given her, Elles having shown the Nightkin inside and then departed. Nemo too was absent, no doubt not wishing to be seen by Karras. Shadows concealed nothing from his kind.

"The company you're keeping surprises me."

Sharna lifted her arms to take in the room. "I didn't really have much choice…besides, I'm working again."

"All of which begs the question, what exactly does *he* have you working on?"

She walked him to where the four Nocturalka lay, nestled together like a clutch of eggs or bizarre fruit. Karras said nothing, only peered at them from a distance as though afraid to come any closer.

"You know what you've got here, don't you?" he managed to keep his voice even.

"You told me you saw one used once."

Karras nodded. "In Orwyn."

"Where's that?"

"Nowhere, now."

"Anything you could tell me would be useful." She made a pouty face. "I'd owe you one."

Karras looked pale, even for one of his breed. "You really mean to use it?" He glanced around the room as if only now aware of where he was. "I see."

He spoke quickly and precisely, telling Sharna exactly what she needed without his usual embellishments or asides. She'd never seen him so agitated; it was almost animal in its intensity.

"Sharna," he said just before he opened the door to leave. "Don't look for me again." Karras looked past her shoulder to where the four incubators sat. "Even *he* won't be able to find me, I promise you." He leaned in close, putting his mouth against her ear. "And if you've any sense, you won't put anything I've said to use."

He was gone before she could ask him why.

She puzzled over her notes, compiling and cross-referencing the information from Karras with what she already had. For the rest of the day after his departure, she'd felt out of sorts. Torn between his cryptic warning and her desire to see this through to the end, regardless of what that might be.

Was that why Nemo had chosen her?

Probably, she reflected. Her tutors always commented on her single-mindedness.

More than once, she knew she should've cut an experiment short, but hadn't. She preferred to live with a string of failed results, rather than let go and never know.

Was this any different?

Don't be stupid, she told herself. It was entirely different, but she had to know what these things did.

She would never get another chance to so much as touch anything so exotic and alien in her life. Even if the university took her back, which was unlikely, they would never be able to match what Nemo offered her.

She doubted she could ever publish a paper on it.

The avenues open in front of her were strictly confined to working on the underside of things. For a long time after her dismissal, though, she'd refused to consider selling her skills on the illicit markets. Back-street flesh mechanics and alterations made to order for some deviant or another did not appeal to her.

What she was doing now was an order of magnitude removed from such acts, but she was fooling herself if she believed it not so very different.

Concentrating on her notes, Sharna pushed the moral arguments out of her mind and focused on the matter at hand. Consequences would come later and she would deal with them as best she could. In the here and now, they were distractions she didn't have the luxury of indulging.

Elles appeared from the shadows with his customary silence after Sharna pulled the small cord hanging near the door. She wondered how he seemed to keep all the hours under the sun and not look done in.

"Yes, Ms. Rae?"

"I need something from the archive."

"Ah, this would be the black archive, would it?"

"Is that a problem?"

He shook his head. "No. It's always best to be clear, though."

"Yes, I suppose it is," Sharna said as she handed him a slip of paper.

Elles unfolded it, turning it left and right in his hands before Sharna moved it so it was the right way up.

"What is it?" He looked unimpressed at the scribble of joined-up lines she'd scrawled.

"An engraving on the item I need."

"And the only way to identify it."

"Yes, and I'm sure it's in the archive. I remember seeing it on my last visit…I think."

"You *think*, or you *know?*"

She thought a moment. "I know."

"What is it exactly?"

"A knife."

Elles turned his eyes briefly on the Nocturalka. "Yes, of course it would be, wouldn't it?"

Workspace tidied, Sharna hefted one of the Nocturalka into place on an empty table. Unseen in the shadows, Nemo watched silently, though Sharna knew he was there. He wasn't likely to miss this, whether it worked or not.

"You're certain?" he asked for the third time.

"Of course I'm not certain," Sharna almost snapped. "But this is probably as close to whatever original method was used to make them work in the first place."

And also about a million or so miles away from it, she didn't say.

"If it doesn't work?"

"Then this priceless specimen will be spoiled."

"I admire your honesty, Ms. Rae."

Dipping her forefinger into a pot of red ink made from crushed insect shells, Sharna carefully and quickly copied the symbols from her notebook. Their meaning was lost on her, save what the ramblings in the original text had provided. All she knew was the order in which they must be applied.

The ink was still drying when she lifted the knife from the floor and slid it free from its sheath.

The blade itself was almost as long as her arm, but aside from its length and the engravings along its side, it looked just like any other knife. The sheath, she had come to understand, was supposed to be made from flayed human skin, though it felt much the same as leather.

Slowly, Sharna brought the tip down towards the Nocturalka. As the tip drew closer, she noticed the black shell quiver ever so slightly—so slightly, in fact, that she wondered if she hadn't imagined it.

The shell split with a sound like wet cloth being torn. A moment later, a gentle breeze sprung up. There was a second of calm and then the breeze turned into a gale, blowing about the room and venting into the cut she'd made.

Whatever Sharna had expected, it wasn't this. She'd crossed over from what she understood of her science and into its most ancient and myth-filled roots. Shamans in caves chanting and frothing at the mouth to re-work the flesh of the faithful.

Steadying herself, she held her free hand over the incision and quickly drew the knife across the bared palm. The blood was pulled towards and into the opening, spattering across the shell and the table.

Slowly, the wind died down to hardly a draught, before it started again—in reverse, this time.

Two red streams snaked and wound around each other from somewhere inside the incision. They were joined by a third, as black as the shell of the Nocturalka itself. Before long all three were entwining and misting, fraying apart like laces to form a cloud just to the left of the table.

The wound in the Nocturalka sealed itself without a sound and the wind stopped with the effect of a window closed on a gale. Boiling, the cloud pulsed once and contracted. Blood spattered to the floor, falling in sheets to leave an unblemished space around what was revealed.

Sharna looked at herself, open-mouthed. She was not so much afraid as curious as to what she saw. It was *her,* but as the other-her stood from its crouch, she saw it wasn't at the same time.

The other-her wore the same clothes, had the same small mole on her left cheek, and even had her hair parted in the same way. Only as she looked closer did she begin to see differences. A slight distending of the hands and fingers, as though the bones underneath the skin were not used to holding such a shape.

There was a hardness around the jaw and she saw something in the eyes she did not like. They were lit by a kind of flinty hunger she herself had never known.

Sharna opened her mouth to speak and the other-her did the same, copying her movements and gestures. Slowly, Sharna walked towards her copy, the other doing likewise. She reached to touch the other-her's face and her doppelganger did the same.

Sharna was surprised to find the skin warm.

The other-her took hold of Sharna's head gently, but firmly, and pressed their foreheads together. What Sharna thought might have been a bifurcated tongue suggested itself behind the other-her's teeth.

Nemo watched as the thing, which he thought of for the moment as Not-Sharna-Rae, dropped the body of its primogenitor to the floor.

Sharna was alive, but only in the most rudimentary of ways. The Unkind one had taken the contents of her head for itself. Slowly, it turned and faced Nemo, no doubt seeing him as clearly as if the entire room was lit by the sun.

"I didn't quite expect this," Nemo explained.

"Your kind never knows what to expect," Not-Sharna said. "It's what makes these moments so enjoyable." It looked down at the prone body by its feet. "She was something. Such a mind," it mused as it tapped its head. "I'm sure I'll sort through it in time."

"I had hoped you would spare her," Nemo's voice had

a trace of what might have been annoyance in it. "She was extremely talented."

"Then she should not have used her own life's blood."

"No matter, it is advantageous to both of us it turned out this way."

"Yes, I take it there is work to do?"

Nemo smiled. "Isn't there always?"

Another Kind

I was a hull rat before I was re-tasked for surface work. Being engineered against vacuum doesn't mean you can stand up to positive atmosphere and hard gravity.

During offload, the crew chiefs started up a double act. I learned later they did it to every new intake, sort of like a ritual to deal with living on Baikalska.

"Hey," one usually started. "When's summer here?"

"Summer?"

"Yeah, like the fucking opposite of winter."

"Winter?"

You probably have to experience Baikalska to get it. The planet's wreathed in a freezing, toxic atmosphere and so far from its star that what passes for daylight is barely enough to see by.

Humans who work on the surface have to wear enviro-suits, and even then can only manage about five-hour rotations outside of the habitats. None of the rats needed expensive gear to survive; we were stamped out for one task, altered for another as needed.

This was the third time I'd been re-tasked, a polite way to describe having your entire body painfully rewritten to fit a new set of environmental circumstances. They say an average rat can manage it maybe five or six times maximum. Burn out follows soon after.

I was still feeling the effects of my last turn; a bone-deep ache that wouldn't go away, as I tramped down the ramp. They don't sugarcoat it. You don't apologize to a tool on the day it snaps, do you?

I shouldn't complain. Eighteen years is old for a rat. Some of the old-timers push twenty and more, but none make to twenty-three.

I hate what I am sometimes, but how can you despise something you never had any control over? Self-loathing can bring a clarity all of its own, after a time.

Baikalska is dotted with sprawling complexes made up of dig sites, processing plants, and refineries. The planet swallows about four thousand rats a solar month, but the return outweighs the cost.

We call it the Grinder. You don't ever want to go there, but you understand that the longer you stay viable, the higher the chance that's exactly where you'll end up. For me, it was easier than onboard ship.

There were a lot of other hull rats like me—and like me, they had the scars on their backs to prove it. Navy arms-men love to beat us as an example of discipline on ship. They take breathing as an infraction when it comes to us.

It felt strange to feel solid ground under my boots instead of subtle vibrations through a deck plate. I couldn't sleep the first week, but the shift rotation put an end to that pretty fast.

To be a slave, you have to be owned. Technically, we weren't anyone's property—but only technically. If we were killed, it wasn't murder, because we weren't human and the law said so. If people thought about us at all, it was simply as tools, components in a machine that was always hungry.

I'd seen a female (Navy ratings call them fuck-bunnies) beaten half to death as a group of men saw to her. Nothing happened then, but she killed herself a week later. The men were reprimanded for causing the loss of a component important to morale.

Compared to that, Baikalska felt like a breeze.

Part of it had to do with its status. I saw it for what it was almost as soon as we touched down and stepped off.

The planet was a hub, maybe *the* hub. Three orbital docks and a space elevator as well as reinforced landing sites for bulk carriers only just able to climb out of the gravity well. About two hundred came and went every day.

Baikalska was a galactic oddity, with enough raw materials to feed the inhabited systems for centuries. You could scrape shale from one of the mountains and still extract something useful.

Beatings slowed things down; they were few and far between. Didn't mean we were free—only humans have that right—but maybe you can see why I was happy to be here and not on a frigate.

I met Ricon after a month on-world. He was a hull rat too, but on merchant ships. I heard they were better, but few of us were tasked to them. Navy always got first dibs on a new litter.

Taller after his last turn and broader through the chest, he worked on the refinery floor. Our paths crossed by chance in the canteen. Even tools needed something to keep them going, right? They fed us a protein-rich gloop that tasted of nothing, which is a feat of engineering in and of itself.

Hardly the most romantic setting to begin a relationship, I know.

The crew chiefs knew we had liaisons, but these had no status. They rationalized it as a kind of imperative. As long as it didn't get in the way of quotas, no one cared.

"You were on ships."

Even turning can't completely hide the paleness and near lack of sclera hull rats pick up.

He took the space across from me. "How long?"

"Five years."

"Only two for me."

He was younger than me, probably about half my age. For us, the older we get, the more it shows.

Black veins stood out along my arms, the skin alabaster white. His were simply pale, and there was a definite trace of white around his iris. My own eyes are like a doll's, lifeless—the better to absorb the limited light in the void.

Each of us are monsters in one way or another, but it takes someone else to see past it

Coming off shift, someone (I'm not sure who) started a whisper that a delegation was coming for an inspection. There was usually one of these every quarter. Normally, it was some official, trailing a gaggle of feeders for the news services.

This time, it was an Advocate.

Saying we were human was technically illegal, the systems having decided that such talk was a danger to the state. Say we're human and then maybe you have to give us rights, or even admit to the possibility that we're equals. We're born, live, and die after all, but that isn't enough to qualify.

She was tall, would've been even without her suit to keep her alive. Her name was Tara Knowles and she seemed genuinely concerned about us, not just playing it up for the liberal minority she maybe hoped to tap for votes in the future.

She spoke to us in groups and individually where she was able. The crew chiefs were nervous about it and hung around her like flies.

One reason they allowed us to have relationships, even if they wouldn't call them that, was to keep us free of agitation. Any spare energy had to be directed to something other than getting worked up about what we were. Her being here, they saw as problematic.

She never spoke to me. Ricon never mentioned if she'd nabbed him for a chat, not that I would've cared over much if he'd have said so.

Change wasn't coming soon. Heard they were talking about classifying anyone who advocated for us as mentally unsound, but that was only talk. Made sense though; arguing for the right of tools can't be a sane line of reasoning, after all.

She left and nothing changed, but the crew chiefs didn't banter so much afterwards. They stopped walking alone on duty and started watching us more closely.

I thought it would pass after a few days.

We were eating in the canteen when a dozen crew chiefs strode in. There was nothing new in that, they came and went all the time as a matter of course. Clustering around the centre of the room, they looked around until they saw our table.

"Something's up," I muttered.

Ricon was playing with his food, trying to find the urge to eat. I wasn't in much better shape. It was usually like that after a shift. You were so hungry, you didn't want to eat.

The lead chief, his name was Brody, tossed something onto the table. Not aimed at anyone in particular, it bounced to a stop at the other end, between plates.

"Mind explaining that?" His voice was cold, even distorted by his speaker grille.

It was a data mine, the kind that can be linked to an external memory grid and used off the 'net. What he was asking wasn't clear and he didn't look to be in the humour to explain—the way he was standing told me as much.

Ricon picked looked at it and then back towards Brody. He shrugged. Brody waved with his glove and the chiefs moved forward, forming a half circle at Ricon's back. The message was clear; whatever Brody was looking for, he thought he'd found it.

I still don't know if there was anything in it, if Ricon might've taken the fucking thing. It was possible; there was always talk among the old-timers of rats who went against the grain. Rumors of cells working to disrupt things, but I'd never met anyone who belonged to one.

Ricon left with them, and I didn't say or do anything to stop him. I never saw him again.

After that, things became hazy. Work, eat, and sleep; repeat.

Grief wasn't something I'd experienced before—ever. Even watching that girl toss herself out of an airlock hadn't brought it out in me. I'd thought it was sad, but that's not the same thing.

I know something in me broke. The things I've done since are enough to convince me that I'm no longer sane.

I was asleep when I rolled over and felt Ricon wasn't there next to me. For a moment, I forgot why, and then it came back. My hand bunched up the cover, gripping hard enough to rip it.

Swinging my legs over the side, I pulled on my overalls and stepped outside. None of the others noticed; too deep in sleep to hear the hatch hiss open and then pop shut behind me.

The complex is never totally quiet, but there are moments when it's more or less still. Pauses between shifts last for whole minutes or more sometimes. It might not sound like much, but in a place like this, they can seem deafening for how quiet they feel.

Overhead, a tender at least a kilometer from bow to stern was rising slowly into the clouds. A twinkling shoal of stars lit along its spine, nearly obscured by the glare of its drives on full burn. As far away as it was, I caught a fragment of the heat wash.

I watched it for a while, until it was almost lost in the cloud cover. Soon, I could only see it by the amber glow of its engines.

"Hey!"

I looked around. A crew chief was jogging towards me; I absently wondered where his partner was. As he got closer, I could see by the way he moved that he was Brody. After a while, we learned to tell them apart.

He came up short and cocked his head. "What are you doing out here? You on shift or something?" His tone was friendly.

Something slid slowly out of place in the back of my head.

"What happened to him?"

"I don't follow."

I heard the smile in his voice. Whatever it was kept on sliding; I could've stopped it, but didn't want to.

"You don't remember?"

"Look, if you're not on shift, you shouldn't be out."

Casual violence is nothing to him, I thought. He'd toss a wrapper away and give about the same thought to beating one of us to death.

When he raised a hand to guide me back to the dorm, I grabbed his wrist hard enough to shatter the bone. Before he could scream, I hit him hard in the throat. I held him by the arm I'd grabbed, and his other hand went to his neck as he did a mad little dance. His feet tapped out a palsied staccato and I heard distorted gurgles through his grille.

I could've smashed his visor or snapped his neck and ended it, but didn't.

The last thing he saw before he stopped moving was my face. I like to think he remembered who I was before he choked to death.

Sometimes when I sleep, curled up under the trees that somehow breathe the poison air, I dream. In the dream, I watch the girl on the ship fly backwards out of the airlock.

The lights strobe warnings and she lowers and then raises her head to look at me. I never helped her; I only followed, and she didn't seem to mind. I think she wanted someone who would remember. *Really* remember, I mean; someone who would know that what she was doing was her choice. Maybe the only free choice she'd made in her life.

Sometimes it's not her face when she looks back up at me, but Ricon's. Sometimes it's a face hidden behind the plate of a suit, one of the many I've killed since I quit the complex.

When they come looking for me, I watch them. Then I kill a few and leave them where they can be found.

They're only visitors to this place—I was made for it. When I go close enough to the complexes to listen, I can hear some of the rats speaking about me. I'm not one of them anymore, so their words don't mean as much as they should.

It's not for them that I kill and hide and run; it's not even for Ricon or the girl. It's not for freedom, because none of us are truly free—not even the crew chiefs. They're governed by a system that holds them in place as much as the others, only they can't ever see it.

I do it because it's my choice. The only choice I can make and the only one that gives me any kind of meaning now.

I am something more than what they made me,

though they think of me as something less. A broken tool that needs to be found and dismantled, no doubt in a painful way if possible; they've been trying for long enough. I am what they made me.

Descent

Selena broke from cover, judging her timing as best she could in the fading light. It was wrong.

The Kynd, a type-two she guessed, not that it meant anything to know what sort it was, drifted overhead. It had no eyes she could see, but was more likely able to perceive in other ways. Most of them could in one way or another.

Extra-sense manifested in most of the first births, which Selena was old enough to remember. Back before it was a problem. Before the Burning.

Its head snapped around, tracking her as she ran. Pieces of debris rose from the ground and trembled until they shattered. At the last moment, she changed direction as the ground in front of her cratered.

She slid around, careful of her footing. She brought her gun up as she came to a stop and fired. The shot was on target and emptied out the Kynd's skull from front to back.

"Shit." She'd hoped to avoid doing it. Finding ammunition was getting harder and harder. One day, the hammer would click on empty...assuming she let it come to that.

Maps meant little these days beyond reminding her of how things used to look, but Selena knew she was near Blackwater.

She remembered coming here as a girl in another life.

Even carpet bombing and cauterizing by orbital projectors couldn't disguise the familiar roll of the hills.

Her last encounter with another survivor was fifteen days behind her, not that it meant much. People tended to stay out of sight these days. The Kynd didn't actively seek them out unless they were foolish enough to present themselves.

Selena supposed they saw little point in finishing a job that humanity had started on itself. A sort of prolonged suicide resulting from the destruction of the land; the slow death of the one world they couldn't share.

When the first riots broke out, followed by control orders, it was too late. The Kynd's existence was no longer a U.S. phenomenon.

She remembered before the 'net finally crashed, but before London or New York (those two always seemed to merge together in her head), there was a post about how they were always born on the same time and the same day. It was one of the last facts she still carried from the Before.

Working out how many children could be born globally kept her mind occupied as she walked.

"A fucking lot, anyway." Talking to herself didn't seem as weird as it did in the beginning; she wasn't sure when she'd started doing it. "Dad used to tell me not to, remember?"

Her father's face was indistinct in her mind, though she was grateful for the detachment. Underneath its protective cover were things she'd forgotten for a reason.

Few useful things were in the past. Like a looter over a corpse, Selena picked clean the things she needed.

Anything left behind could stay where it was.

The brain could remember without much effort, she found. The muscle's inactivity was unequal to the task of actively shedding its surplus weight, no matter how much she did or didn't try. She knew being close to Blackwater was the cause. Selena didn't plan to stay long.

The town was more intact than she'd expected it to be. One or two buildings were still standing, and they were easily the tallest things she'd seen in months. They looked alien, as though dumped on a blasted landscape from the sky. She eyed them, feeling as though they were returning the favor.

"Little green men might come pouring out, ray guns in hand," she said and smiled to herself.

On the road nearby, burned-out wrecks formed twisted reefs tarred black by intense fire. Some she could see still had bodies in them and a few were almost melted into each other in a way suggestive of a magneto or kinetic Kynd.

The names were pulled from pop culture references when they still meant something. Now they were meaningless signposts, only useful for simple reference points. Naming them didn't make Selena think of them as human, never mind if they came from human wombs or not. They were another species—another Kynd.

The 'i' being exchanged for a 'y' came from some blog she'd caught. The last viral post before things really went bad.

Following the line of wrecks, Selena made her way

down a gradual slope into town. If asked, she wouldn't be able to say why she was here. It only seemed like a good idea, but it felt unclean somehow. Like scrabbling over a rotting body or two; the memories of the past tried to surface, giving it the air of desecration.

"There's nothing holy here." It sounded true, even if gods of a sort had inherited the earth.

The ratchet of a slide made her stop. Selena moved her hand as slowly as she could to the gun resting in its webbing against the small of her back.

No one shouted for her to stop, so they maybe didn't have a clear view of her. That would change fast.

He stepped from behind cover, rifle casually raised. The barrel took a turn towards the ground as he stepped closer. Long hair and months' worth of beard went some way to hiding his age, but as he neared Selena, she guessed him to be no more than thirty-five. Only his eyes carried a greater age, brittle and hollowed-out like those of an alcoholic. Like she knew her own must look.

"Got any food?"

He slung his rifle and stopped. "Some."

"Some," she repeated. It would do. As introductions went, it wasn't bad.

He turned and started walking back the way he'd come. Selena took it as a cue she could follow.

His name was Martin. He told her he'd been in Blackwater for about two weeks, mostly scavenging what was left in the town.

"Haven't seen anyone else since I got here," he said as he stirred the pot over the fire. They were inside one of the buildings. Though hollow for the most part inside, it was pretty much in one piece otherwise. "Seen one or two Kynd."

"Killed one a ways back," she said and described how in a handful of words.

"You killed many?" The question would've been unthinkable in the Before, but this was the Now.

"Fifth one."

Selena might have taken pride in it, if she could remember how to. A lot of others had, before the Burning. TV shots of mobs pulling whole families out into the street, going door to door with guns or homemade clubs.

"I try to avoid them, but feels like it's getting harder to manage."

"There's no pattern to how they move. Sometimes it's like they don't really see us."

"They see us."

"You ever wonder how they changed so fast?" he asked as he poked the fire, scattering sparks into the air.

Selena wasn't really listening, only nodding out of a programmed habit her father gave to her to appear she was paying attention. She'd given up trying to figure things out a long time ago, but it seemed Martin wasn't at that point yet.

He doled out the stew into a pair of battered cups. While it wasn't all that good, it was the best hot meal she'd enjoyed for a while.

"You wonder what the point of any of it was?"

"How do you mean?" she asked as she sipped, dimly wishing for some bread to dip into her cup.

"Everything we did or didn't do," Martin said as he uncrossed his legs and stretched out. "All the things we worried about. Global warming, gays marrying and adopting, the economy." He leaned back on his elbows. "None of it was important in the end, was it?"

"It would be my luck to find a nihilist, wouldn't it?"

"Never said that, but all of it seems like fuck-all now, don't you think?"

Selena gave him that much at least, though she didn't want to encourage him to bring up more of the past. Not here. All of its petty worries were just that—petty and small. They only really mattered so long as there was someone around to consider them.

Wall Street had little meaning if it was a corpse-choked avenue.

Cradling her cup, Selena looked around slowly, surveying the place Martin had set up for himself. "You look pretty comfortable here."

"Didn't take long." He refilled his cup and offered more to her. "Figure I'll be sad to go."

Nothing was permanent now, human contact least of all. Selena accepted the food.

Something picked at the back of her mind. His reluctance to leave seemed too forced, like he was trying to mask something else. Then she realized he might just be making himself say it to remind himself he would have to go one day soon.

Selena put it down to tiredness and fading people

skills. Being in company again could do that, in her experience.

Night was difficult to get used to now. It was so still. Without the comfort of streetlights, everything took on a very different quality.

Selena imagined this was how people felt before they'd learned to build houses. Moving across plains until they stopped and made what shelter they could, where they could.

The fire was burning down to embers. She appreciated its warmth and the feeling of security it provided. Of course, both feelings were only in her head to one degree or another, but neither felt less real because of it.

Glancing around, it took her a moment to realize Martin was gone. The firelight caught the edge of his bedroll, enough to show it was empty.

Selena wasn't surprised he was gone. The more she thought about it, the more a lot of his setup here didn't make sense. He'd been here too long already, it seemed, to show any signs of leaving soon.

Whatever was keeping him here was his business, but Selena was already thinking it over.

"Shit, you're not even really sure it *is* anything, are you?"

She'd become rusty with people to the point where reading them felt like an almost archaic action. It was useful once, but now redundant on all but the most basic level.

Was someone going to kill or help you? Beyond that, you didn't need to understand other motivations.

They wanted to help you because it was the logical way to survive. They wanted to kill you for the same reason. Unspoken between Selena and Martin were the people they'd either helped or killed.

"No need to mention the seven men and women you put down along with the five Kynd, is there?" she spoke almost in a giggle, the voice something like her own.

Martin would be able to guess what she'd needed to do in order to survive. She was perfectly able to guess about him.

"It's not hard to imagine what can happen up here," she said, tapping her temple gently.

Talking about it solved nothing. It was just life in the Now.

When she did think about it, Selena thought about how it was probably the last thing the Kynd had taken from the survivors. They at least weren't human, and while the survivors might think themselves people still, they were only animals running around in the shit.

Fate and the futility of human endeavor were useless things to chew over. Selena remembered being a lawyer, but it felt like it had happened to someone else.

Hazy light flashed around in the dark, bobbing in a way that told her Martin was coming back. She turned away from the fire, listening as he entered the building. There was something slightly off about his footsteps, but she didn't stay awake long enough to listen.

Morning was grey, like it was most mornings. The fallout and debris in the atmosphere cut the sunlight and temperature both. Martin was cooking meat over the rekindled fire. The smell had woken her.

"What's that?"

"The reason I've stayed so long," he said, cutting a piece and tossing it over. "Deer. There aren't many I've seen, but enough to make me hold out and stay."

Made sense why he was gone last night, at least.

Questions lost a lot of their importance as Selena ate. The meat was hot and she tried to be careful about burning her tongue, then stopped caring and let it happen anyway.

Martin cut a piece for himself. "Didn't seem right not to say."

Selena would've appreciated his decency, but at the moment she was only grateful for the chance to eat something that wasn't out of a can or packet. It didn't stir any memories, but it satisfied her in a way that what she'd grown used to couldn't do.

That was memory enough, in its own way.

"How many have you found?" she asked, rubbing her slightly raw tongue against the roof of her mouth.

"Not many, not enough to call a herd, anyway."

"I've barely seen a bird all this time."

Martin shifted where he sat, as though uncomfortable in a way that had nothing to do with his position.

"When I came here, I was...ready. You know?" He mimed what he meant, a finger to the side of his head and the thumb as the hammer of an imagined or real gun.

She'd thought often enough about what she might do with her last bullet; her days were measured against the things she killed.

"That's when I saw it. Kind of made me think twice."

"Sometimes that's all you need. A reason to think twice." Selena wondered how many moments like that she'd be able to find. "You'll have to show me."

Something crossed his face for a second. "Thought you'd say that," he said and offered a smile. "Not yet."

Sentiment or some kind of ideology, however loose, which he'd built up, maybe? She wanted to believe that was it, though the look on his face gave her pause all the same.

Climbing the ruined ladder, Selena made it up to the roof of the building. Seen from outside, she'd assumed there was no way up.

A day and a night had proved her wrong.

From where she stood, the desolation around her looked near total. The ground looked blacker, charred like ash, and dense clumps of skeletal trees covered the hills in places.

"What would deer live on out here?" They might've changed over time, she thought. Adapting to their new environment as the survivors did.

Selena was unable to reconcile the meat she'd tasted with the Now as it was. It was from a healthy, well-fed animal. Once the satisfaction faded, the questions came back.

Movement among the trees drew her eye.

'Martin.' She mouthed the word rather than giving voice to it. She could see a carcass draped across his shoulders. "No shot to mark the kill."

It was possible he used traps to save his bullets,

though.

Selena ducked down and left the roof by the way she'd come. There was a way out the front where she could slip around so he couldn't see her.

For all its lifelessness, the forest was thicker in places than she'd expected. Selena was some ways in before she realized it actually was a forest and not just a desiccated clump like the rest.

Didn't matter; she remembered the direction Martin had come from.

She wasn't sure what she expected to find. Evidence of snares or whatever, but the deeper she went into the forest, the more she doubted she would find anything. There was nothing green anywhere. Selena couldn't remember the last time she'd seen a living plant.

Absently, she pulled her gun from its web nest.

Part of her hoped she was wrong; the part of herself that still dwelt in the past. The bigger part of her, the part in the Now, knew she was right.

Nothing about this made sense—and that was saying something with the way things were.

The girl was maybe fourteen. Tall for her age and thin, with long, dark hair.

Selena saw her from behind and froze. She'd half lowered her gun when the girl turned. She brought it back up.

Her eyes.

Selena saw it in her eyes. The mark all the Kynd

shared.

A branch snapped behind her and the cold barrel of Martin's rifle pressed against the back of her neck.

"Did she call you?"

"She can when she needs to."

Couldn't he see it? The mark, it was there. Did he see something else?

If he'd kept her chained up out here, she could understand that. Maybe. She could understand anything but this. It was inside his head and he'd allowed it in there.

"That's not all she can do, is it?"

"No, she can shift things."

Keep him talking. "Shift?"

"It's what she calls it. Bringing things into reality from…wherever." The barrel trembled a little. He moved his feet to steady himself. "She saved me."

"Is that what you believe?"

"She's not like the others. They don't want her."

It didn't change anything, even if it was true.

"Put the gun down."

The girl looked dirty and worn around the edges. Her thinness looked more the result of hunger than anything to do with her height.

No! The Kynd weren't like that…were they?

Could she be inside two heads at once? Would Selena know if she was inside hers?

She raised her gun a fraction.

Martin pressed his rifle in, digging into the skin so it hurt. "Don't."

It wasn't going to be her last bullet after all.

Selena pulled the trigger.

Of the Blood

The monsters cried in their sleep, the one facet of their humanity that Namael's ministrations couldn't burn away. They understood what they were and what they had been.

It was a curious thing and he'd devoted days to dissection, testing, and note taking in an effort to understand the cause. In the end, no clear answer presented itself.

His lab—some would say lair—lay beneath the Autarch's tower, almost exactly in the centre of Carcosa. In the halls above, courtiers and nobles would be cavorting or else languidly enjoying the many other pleasures on offer.

Namael was never invited to the revels, his presence like as not would dampen the spirit of the occasion. A reminder of what could befall any one of those above, should they displease the Autarch.

He remembered one young fop who'd made the mistake of tripping a servant, sending both the man and the tray of crystal glasses he carried crashing to the floor. Not in itself an unusual thing to happen, but it spoiled the mood during a performance by Nurisa Vak, the effect being that the orgiastic inducement of her aria was ruined.

The fop in question slumbered fitfully in one of the end cages, due for the fighting pits before too long. His newly worked flesh gave him a physicality more suited to his blundering nature.

Reaching under his mask, the death mask of his old teacher, Namael scratched the side of his nose with one boney finger. A monster jerked in its sleep, arms paddling like a dog's. The fleshmaker couldn't recall if it had been a man or woman before he'd seen to it, and its current form was devoid of such binaries as gender.

A door banged open somewhere, the sound echoing down the labyrinth of chambers leading to his sanctum. None of the monsters woke, each too much in the grip of their nightmares and memories of their past lives.

Gradually, footsteps became audible as Shya drew closer. He knew it was her; he could hear the distinctness of her walk, though a casual listener wouldn't have been able to. Almost a century in each other's company meant he could pick out the scent of the oil that she used on her hair, even from so great a distance.

Theirs was an intimacy somewhere above that of lovers, but altogether something different.

Another smell crept ahead of her, lacing itself under the odors of the room. Almost sweet, there was a hard tang buried within it—witchery. Shya was of the blood, and the aethyr was literally in her veins. It was why he'd chosen her to work with from so many who jumped at the chance.

She came into the chamber, the air hissing softly around her. Sparks danced faintly along the cage bars.

"You've been busy tonight," he said.

"No more than usual," she said, lifting one hand and making a show of examining her nails. Like all those of her kind, her skin was the color of glacier ice.

A thin faced defined by sharp features that would put

a weapon smith to shame, the most striking thing about her were her eyes. Each was red, as though filled with enough blood to burst. Though nominally human, she was of a different order, changed from birth in a way beyond even his skill.

"Anything worth telling?"

"Couple of deaths on the street of blades."

"Nothing worth using?"

She shook her head. "A crowd went into a frenzy and tore apart what was left."

"Let me guess…they came from Madam Kallin's?"

She dipped her head by way of an answer.

"Kallin always did enjoy pushing things." Namael's eyes glazed over for a moment, dimly recalling another time.

"The city's starting to jump," Shya said, waving a hand through the air. "Every festival, it seems to start earlier and earlier."

He conceded she was probably right, as far as he knew about such things.

The Masque always drove Carcosa to breaking point, a little more so every year. Always a little wilder, the last one stretching even the hedonistic limits of the Autarch.

"This is different." Her already sharp features hardened, seeming to grow edges. "The aethyr is disturbed."

Namael cocked his head in interest. "How so?"

"The currents are shifting, much more so than usual."

Obsidian flecks danced across Shya's eyes. She peered into the aethyr, a thin layer of frost spreading across her arms and face.

"There are voices, too," Shya sounded distant, literally

as if she was speaking from far away.

"What do they say?"

Blinking tears out of her eyes, she closed the window only she could open. The frost crackled and melted, falling to the floor in fast-dissolving chips. "I can't say exactly, but they're getting closer."

A new specimen was strapped to the wheel, an apparatus his mentor had designed to break and reset bones as quickly as possible. Namael mixed Shya's donated blood with several of his own concoctions. After so many decades at this, he no longer heard his subjects scream.

No one said what the man had done to warrant Namael's attentions, and he never bothered to ask.

Leaning over the man's shattered legs, he made a small incision with a paper-thin scalpel and dipped a needle into the mix. Once it was applied, the skin around the wound began to ripple and churn as the change came on. Should the process work, the Autarch would have a fearsome specimen indeed for his private display.

Leaving his subject writhing in place, Namael crossed to one of his many paper-strewn desks. He leafed through the sheets, but his mind was still pondering Shya's news.

He was old enough to remember the last shreds of collective gossip about something called the Conjunction. In those days, the stories were almost whispers, and now they were nothing at all.

With the Masque approaching, he had enough to occupy himself. The Magisters each wanted a dozen specimens for the festival—the absolute most he could create. Such a production, Namael calculated, would require a visit to one or two prisons.

What did it mean? Conjunction was a word adrift, without context; it was something any idiot might babble. Yet, tasting it on his tongue, he felt its promise of something.

He glanced over at the subject. The man's lower body was entirely reformed; the legs now more like the stalk limbs of a mantis, though each ended in something like a hoof.

Walking around the wheel, he took hold of the man's head. The eyes would have to go, but implanting another sight organ wasn't an issue. He decided he would forgo another crown; symbol of Carcosa or not, he fancied something different that would satisfy the Autarch.

Shya's own heartbeat deafened her for a moment before it began to return to normal. The rhythm gradually lessened, until one beat came whole minutes after another.

Her eyes, normally red, filled with black. The color bloomed like ink dropped into water as she slipped fully into the aethyr. Nothing mattered here. Any sense of reference there was solely in her mind. The aethyr took on a form she could in some way grasp; it was a riotous mess of colors, which rose and surged in great waves. It was what she expected, so that was what it was.

The voices were still here, closer than before, but meaningless all the same. Another presence ghosted nearby, drifting elegantly to her side.

"Izair," she greeted him, but didn't bother to look his way.

"How's life with the deadsoul?" Blunt as ever, he smirked at his own humour.

"He has a soul, as we all do."

"One so deadened to sense that nothing could wake it."

She was tempted to banish him. They both knew she could do it, and Izair must have picked up on some subtle shift in her aura. He let himself drift a little away from her.

"We can all hear them, not just you," he said, waving a hand vaguely.

"I'd be surprised if few couldn't."

"It doesn't mean anything good."

Shya snorted. "Expert now, are you?" In truth, she felt it too, but hearing Izair give voice to private dread was laughable.

He offered a mock bow. Shya wondered if normal folk knew that she and her kind were like them in more ways than were at first apparent.

No one could say what caused the emergence of the Blood Born. The first generation endured a frenzied pogrom before they were sought alive for the entertainment of various Autarchs. Now, they went unmolested about the city, hiring themselves out to whomever they wanted. Only the Autarch could be said to truly stand above them.

Shya contemplated, not for the first time, that she had no memory of her father. There was only a vague impression of a very tall figure. She supposed she'd been smaller back then, but couldn't reconcile the idea with the feeling that he'd really been that big.

Turning her attention back Izair, she found he'd

drifted still further away.

"If your feeling is so strong, Izair, then we should summon a Gathering," she told him. She might loathe the man, but his intuition was second to none. Shya supposed it made up for his other deficiencies.

"I couldn't agree more," he said over his shoulder. "Hope you find time in your day, I hear the fleshmaker keeps you busy."

Servants, their eardrums pierced so they couldn't hear what was said, went about the business of cleaning the Autarch's hall. Namael ignored them as he padded into the presence of Carcosa's ruler.

He was seldom—if ever—summoned, and was often content not to be. The Autarch was the only being Namael could say he feared. He was ancient by most reckonings, but showed no sign of age. Namael suspected he was altered in some way he couldn't understand and sometimes, in his darker moments, wondered how to contrive a sample from the Autarch.

He was a giant of a man, though to one as stooped as Namael, everyone looked bigger to one degree or another

He was naked from the waist up; his thickly muscled body was extensively tattooed. Interlocking swirls and coiled serpents writhed their way up his arms and over his shoulders. The centre of his chest was inked—some said in blood—with an imperial crown of antlers, which gradually flowed into the shape of a tree.

Legend went that the Autarchs took the symbol after winning a great, though long forgotten, victory. Hardly surprising in Carcosa, where most memory only went as far back as the last Masque.

The Autarch's face was concealed behind a mirrored oval, which he never removed in the presence of any, save for the Sightless.

Namael occasionally had to create more of them, the blind menials who tended the master of Carcosa in private. It wasn't as simple as removing the eyes, but required epidermal and nerve grafts to heighten physical sensitivity and aural enhancement. They typically expired from sensory overload.

"Namael," his voice was soft, faintly womanly. "I apologize for the state of my hall." He gestured to a servant busily scrubbing some sort of bodily fluid from the floor. "Our revels never seem to end."

"As you say, Eminence." Namael offered a bow.

"Come closer," the Autarch said, waving him forward.

As he ascended the steps, the scent of sweet oils and sweat filled his nostrils. He stopped on the second to last step, a mixture of respect and fear holding him in place.

"How go your preparations for our Masque?"

"Well enough, Eminence." The thought occurred to him to mention Shya's news, but he decided against it. What difference could bringing it up make?

"Anything you need, you have but to ask," the Autarch said, rising and casting his shadow over Namael. Slowly, he leaned closer to the fleshmaker.

At such a distance, Namael caught the whiff of something from behind the oval mask. Sweet like figs, but heavy like wine, it seemed to draw him forward against his reason.

Cupping Namael's chin, the Autarch raised his face upwards, as gentle as a lover might. "Anything you need, Namael," he cooed as a mother would to an infant. "I want nothing spared."

Chewing the inside of his cheek to ward off trembling, Namael gently brushed the back of the Autarch's hand. He knew from experience that the gesture was looked for at such times.

"I serve, Eminence."

"Your company would be welcomed here. There are those who would submit willingly to your touch."

Namael swallowed. The offer was an old one, but the temptation was a dangerous distraction. This place, while a place of revelry, was a den of lust and avarice. He was as likely to end up with a knife in the back as anything else.

"I will consider it, Eminence." It was the answer he always gave.

The Autarch withdrew his hand and returned to his throne. "I mustn't keep you from your work."

With that, Namael took his leave, backing down the steps and ignoring the Deafened, who continued to work in silence as he passed.

Shya peered down through a skylight. In the room below, a couple were doing unspeakable things to each other. They seemed to be enjoying it, despite the blood. Sometimes she wondered how this city could function, but decided trying to puzzle it out would drive her insane.

A muscle in her back twinged, tightening enough to

make her flinch. She turned at the same moment a hand reached through from nowhere, pulling the body it was attached to into reality from nonexistence.

A cluster of misshapen ram's horns curved back from its skull, framing a face inlaid with black symbols.

Shyal knew a riele when she saw one, though she'd not yet been born the last time one was sighted in Carcosa. She stepped back, conscious of her footing on the roof tiles. The disturbance of the creature's entry caused the sky to split with a single peal of thunder, followed by the first drops of rain a moment later.

Huffing, the riele sniffed the air and licked out with a bifurcated tongue. Its eyes blazed emerald green, seemingly lit from within. Shya knew the light there came from somewhere else.

It regarded her, bobbing its head from side to side. She raised her hand, clawing it into the beginnings of a warding gesture. She wasn't sure if she could banish it, but hoped it wouldn't come to that. She knew almost nothing about them, save for the ghosts of memories caught on eddies and currents in the aethyr.

"Blood Born," its teeth clicked as it spoke. "Born of blood, yes yes, but you know not whose."

"What are you talking about?"

It tried on something like a smile. "He learned from his own father, though his children remember him not."

It stepped closer, but Shya held her ground. What she'd taken for a wet animal musk was the reek of the aethyr in its purest form. It made her want to gag, but she bit back on it.

"Look for his sign, if you have eyes to see."

Before Shya could ask another question, it slashed a hand through the air, which rippled the way oil does on water. The slash spread vertically, forming a rough black line.

The riele stepped through and the tear sealed behind it, its closing drawing another snap of thunder from the sky.

Namael picked over his subject's exposed nerve endings, satisfied with the growth of the new grafts. The threat of rejection was always an issue, more so with basilisk tissue. The unfortunate might have cried out, if not for the removal of his vocal chords.

Unhappy with his earlier work, Namael had returned the legs to their previous shape before undertaking more subtle work. Shaving skin and muscle, he managed to elegantly flay entwined designs into the flesh. Thinner now than before, it was necessary to add additional bone segments to compensate for what was missing. The subject's shoulders and chest were bulked out in disproportion to his slender waist, the body taking the shape of an hourglass.

Namael locked a vice closed, gripping the head in place. He peered down into what was left of his subject's face, where the eyes used to be. Nothing in his collection suited what he had in mind for the head.

Wheels creaking, he pulled a portable easel within reach and started sketching with a nub of charcoal. He'd already discarded a dozen designs, but nothing seemed to fit together. Each time it seemed as if a solution was within reach, but before Namael could realize it, it flitted away.

Against his earlier thought, he decided antlers would do after all—but not the traditional crown of Autarch. Instead, he wanted to fashion something older, something more archaic, to capture the spirit of the Masque.

If legend was right, the Masque itself was older than Carcosa. An ancient ritual, the true symbolism of which had faded over time to become the orgy it was now.

Namael's problem was a lack of reference; nothing remained of those days. Carcosa was too consumed in the here and now—a city without history and losing more of its memory all the time in the pursuit of baser things.

He needed sleep, but couldn't bring himself to chance it.

The paper in front of him rippled as a small breeze wafted through the chamber. No wind ever reached down this far. Turning, Namael found a creature standing near the opposite end of the wheel. Though it was outwardly human, the fleshmaker recognized something *other* when he saw it.

Neither he nor she, it was perfectly androgynous. White hair fell to its shoulders, framing a face so symmetrical that even Namael found it uncomfortable to look at, despite its apparent beauty.

"Your work is not without merit," its voice was melodic, shifting in pitch from masculine to feminine. "A remaker of form and kind, yet your own body leaves much to be desired."

Surprisingly, Namael found himself becoming

aroused. His member, long out of use, began to stir.

"I try my best."

"You appear to have hit a stumbling block," it said, moving around the wheel to Namael's side, though he wasn't aware of it doing so. "You need to think of your subject as a vessel, not as a canvas."

"A vessel for what?"

"Whatever may so inspire you."

It lifted a long-fingered hand and pushed back strands of Namael's iron-grey hair. A tremor passed through his skull and he fought back the urge to cry out.

"You thought yourself immune to feeling?"

"I did."

It gestured to the subject. "You think he is?"

Namael knew he wasn't. All of his subjects crossed a threshold, a point where pain transmuted into something else. If not quite its antonym, it at least came close. Only the memories lingered, like phantom limbs.

"Nor are you incapable of dreams, as you think you are." Wiping a hand over the paper, it smeared Namael's drawing. "Sleep, fleshmaker," it said as it turned to leave by whatever means it had used to arrive. "We will meet again before the end."

Not all the Blood attended the Gathering. They were informal things and the Blood were an informal caste. Age and ability were respected, but there was no true rank among them. Being of a kind after a fashion, it was more like a meeting between family members.

There were the twins, Anya and Tulane, and Haldon.

Shya thought he must be eighty now, at least. She'd believed him dead a long time, but wasn't the first to assume so. Izair was among the last to appear. There were ten all told, about what she'd expected.

"You managed to pull yourself away?" Izair offered a sneer, trying to bait her. She wasn't in the mood for a sparring match.

"Go fuck a pig." His eyes hardened. Vulgarity was seldom appreciated among them.

"You have something to tell us, Shya?" Haldon's voice was soft, but carried undercurrents of old power. The air seemed to buckle under each syllable.

"A riele," she stated, keeping half an eye on Izair and waiting for a snide remark that never came.

"All of us felt it."

"Strange it should come to you," Tulane said.

"I was near the centre of the storm," she told them, remembering what it had said. She chewed her tongue out of habit.

"The storm broke as a result of the aethyr's unrest," Izair said evenly.

"A bleed?"

"It would seem so," replied Anya.

None of them had ever seen a riele in the flesh before, and Shya realized each was staring at her in turn.

"How was it?" Haldon asked.

"Strange." That was saying something for Carcosa.

"It means nothing good," Izair added.

"The voices are getting closer," Tulane said.

They looked to Haldon, but there was no answer

there, and none of the others so gathered looked to be in the way of offering anything either. This was beyond them.

"The Autarch is taken up with the Masque," Shya reminded them. "Nothing will distract him from it."

"He must feel it," Izair snorted.

"He does," Haldon cut in. "But as Shya said, he will not be drawn."

"It falls to us, then?"

Shya wondered if Carcosa was worth saving from whatever was coming and reluctantly decided it was. There was no sense of love or loyalty for the place, but it was all she and the others knew.

The city had the protectors it deserved, gods help it.

Namael's dreams were disturbed. Whether through the shifts in the aethyr or the androgyne's touch, he wasn't sure. He knew that when the aethyr was in flux, it could seep into the real, able to find purchase in dreams.

He was in Carcosa, though it was different from how it really was. He recognized the mason's square, though much of it was in ruins.

Down one street, a tall shadow passed across a wall. Namael followed, always turning a corner in time to see it drift around another bend in the street.

As he walked, dream logic prevented him from running; he glanced up at the sky. Black stars danced close to the moons. Each bled shadows into the sky, forming a wreath around something ill-defined overhead.

When he looked back, the shadow's owner stood in the middle of the street.

It was no trick of the light or fallacy of the dream; it was as tall as its shadow suggested. Dirty yellow robes hung from a wire-thin body like rags draped over driftwood.

It turned slowly around, revealing a face concealed behind a black mask. A crown of thorns and branches worked into the semblance of antlers adorned its head. A runic sign appeared to be woven in among the tangle, but refused to define itself when Namael tried to focus on it.

He couldn't move. Dream logic rooted him to the spot, but it was more than that. He knew with a certainty found only in the subconscious that this creature was known to him, or would be.

Its form carried echoes of what little he knew of the earliest Masques. The crown adorning its head was just that: a crown for a king, clothed in yellow.

It raised one arm, the tattered robes falling away to reveal a skeletal limb the color of charred rock. Its hand opened, the fingers splaying spider-limb wide.

Namael woke, eyes coming open at once and the feeling of the dream tight in his chest. Already the form of the king was fading, only the abstract remained; a feeling that was not quite a memory of what he'd seen.

The king was a signifier, but the shifting symbol was the key. Such a thing was outside his skill to fashion, but the attempt was worth it.

The king meant something primal, animalistic. While Namael had never attended one, he understood the Masques and their staleness of late; always lost in a slick haze of oiled bodies and drug smoke that passed for what they were supposed to be.

They filled a place in the calendar, nothing more. Carcosa had never been on the right path, he wasn't fool enough to think it, but something was missing.

Rising, he crossed through to his lab, separated from his bedroom by a thin curtain.

His subject lay where he'd left him. Coming to his head, Namael drew a sheet and pinned it in place on the easel.

He wasn't surprised when the androgyne appeared again. Was it part of the dream? Was he in fact dreaming still?

"No, fleshmaker. Few things separate the waking world and what lies within," it said as it tapped the side of its head.

"There's more sense there," Namael replied, not taking his eyes from the drawing taking shape on the paper.

"The sign will elude you."

Namael paused and leaned around the easel to face it.

"It is within us all, had you but eyes to see it."

"How?"

"You must learn."

It had something to show him, Namael saw as much. Setting his charcoal down, he lingered long enough to pull a cloak over himself before following after it.

As far as Shya could tell, there were no other sightings of riele in the city. Whether that was good or bad, she'd no way of knowing.

Carrion as they were, it was possible they were simply circling beyond sight. The aethyr was disturbed enough that they could conceal themselves with little effort. More disturbing was the thinning she sensed.

The barrier between the aethyr and the real was wearing down in places. It was as though someone was rubbing fabric between forefinger and thumb, eroding both sides at a more or less equal rate.

The voices on the currents were almost clear now, but spoke over one another, remaining impenetrable.

It wouldn't last, but she feared what she would hear when they were understandable. She was also drawn to whatever message they carried.

Carcosa itself was reacting in different ways. The thinning of reality made people act out in unusual ways, not that much was considered beyond the pale here. Still, she noticed a pushing of what few limits there were. There were more bodies turning up in the canal, especially where it emptied into Lake Hali.

Shya padded by the shore, careful not to disturb things any more than they were already.

The lake surface was still and as flat as unbroken glass. She could sense the tremors beneath. Something was probing at the edge of things, trying to be subtle about it. Moving as close to the water as she dared, Shya peered at a body near where the sand and shingle met the grass.

She was fresh, this one—probably dead no more than a day. The same sign was carved on her exposed skin. Like the others, it was edged in yellow ink or dye.

Its meaning was lost on her. Almost runic, it suggested a crooked cross, but seemed to change shape if she looked at it for too long.

If the riele were responsible, they did this without being seen. While possible, she doubted it. From what she knew of them, it wasn't their way of doing things. Bottom feeders seldom went for live prey.

The sign continued to move, reworking itself over and again whenever Shya looked at it. Blinking didn't make it stop, so she screwed her eyes shut until it hurt. When she opened them again, the woman was standing.

A wound on her neck cracked wide, what scab there was splitting as dry bark might. Stilled blood dribbled out, so thick it was practically black.

Her eyes looked jaundiced, but Shya might have been wrong. Half of the sign was carved brutally onto her left cheek; the bone showed through whitely in places.

While she knew she was still near Lake Hali, Shya also knew she was elsewhere, as though she'd crossed the shore somehow to the other side. A weight nudged against her chest and something tugged at her legs.

"We are all of us his angels," the dead woman said. "But you alone are his children."

"Whose children?"

"Him, we all know him, but you are his child. How could you forget him?"

The dead woman was in front of Shya, but neither one of them had moved. She pressed her lips to Shya's, and the Blood Born let the woman's tongue find hers.

She felt its dry roughness and tasted the iron/coppery tang of old blood. Nevertheless, she leaned into it. Things suddenly shifted and the woman was where Shya first saw her, lying dead on the shore.

A sense of first dis- and then re-location hit her. Swaying, Shya managed to catch herself before falling.

Glancing at the lake, she sensed the shifting thing beneath the waters was still, its attention now focused on her.

Namael didn't recognize this part of Carcosa, but that was far from worrysome. He supposed the city must have changed much in the intervals between his outgoings.

The androgyne did not walk so much as drift. Its feet made no sound and didn't even look to be moving beneath its robes. He followed it down a rat's warren of streets; the buildings leaned in over them, their lit windows regarding them curiously.

"Where are we?" he finally asked.

"Carcosa," was all the answer it offered.

The street opened out into a small square. An ancient-looking tree rose through the stones at its centre, towering almost as high as the looming buildings. Namael didn't think there were any trees in Carcosa, despite what he could see in front of him.

This wasn't Carcosa. Even the air felt different, yet the Autarch's tower was still visible as it always was, no matter where one stood in the city.

"The theatre's just over here."

"Theatre?"

"That's what I said."

"I know enough about theatres in Carcosa," he said. *Too much,* he sometimes thought. "I've no wish to see such primitive mutilation."

"This is not like any theatre you've heard of, I assure you."

They came to a building with sagging walls. Someone had daubed a scrawl above the door in yellow paint. It was a shade of the color he couldn't remember seeing before.

'*Irrealitie,*' it said. The paint ran in places, dripping down the facade in thick streaks.

"The act of remaking the body is one of irreality, is it not?"

Namael considered it. He'd thought of his work only in clinical terms, never pausing to consider its possible philosophical implications.

"A body of one and many parts, and all parts of that body, being many, are one," the androgyne said as it looked at him, its eyes unreadable.

"Is that from a book?"

"Paraphrasing, and it hasn't been written yet. We should go inside, the performance is about to begin."

Later, Namael would be unable to fully grasp what he'd seen. He was left only with the impression he'd somehow stepped back into the dream as the troupe manipulated a life-sized puppet like the thing he'd followed through the other Carcosa.

It wasn't exactly the same as he'd dreamed, but it was close enough to make him again ask if he was still asleep.

At some point in the play, a woman came on stage. She wore only a filmy dress and a pallid mask. Looking over at the androgyne, he saw it was wearing one too. Sitting so close, Namael took pains to hide his growing erection. Gently, the androgyne reached over and turned Namael's face back towards the stage before sliding its hand downwards.

After that, everything stopped—and when things started again, he was alone in his chambers. His subject was still in place, still waiting to be finished.

Shya felt things were coming to some kind of head. Rather than becoming discernable, the voices riding the aethyr were even more confusing than before.

A heavy calm was settling over Carcosa, contradicting the frenzy within the elsewhere. The eye of a storm was crawling over the city, promising a gale to follow.

The other Blood Born stayed in contact infrequently. When she met them, she didn't mention her experience at the lake. If they'd gone through anything similar, they kept it to themselves.

She doubted they had, but couldn't say why. Something in their eyes betrayed their ignorance. There was nothing lurking around the edge of their pupils.

Since the lake, whenever she caught her reflection in glass along a street or on some rooftop, Shya caught sight of something at the edge of it. Whenever she turned or tried to keep her eye on it, whatever it was vanished as if it was never there—and she wasn't sure it had been.

It left not so much as a flutter behind, suggesting a level of power she couldn't fathom.

So far, it was content only to follow, but Shya doubted it would stay that way forever. It took no notice of distance in its watching. One glimpse put it on the other side of the street and another within arm's reach.

She turned down an alley she knew dead-ended not far from the south boundary wall. The play was an obvious one, but Shya knew directness was the only way out of some situations.

Turning, she saw it wasn't there, but she knew it wouldn't be. She completed her turn, coming to a stop facing the wall at the end of the alley.

The figure in front of her was tall enough to dwarf the Autarch and while its shape was sexless, it tended towards the feminine. 'Her' face was blank, secreted behind what Shya took to be a mask so seamlessly fitted, it could've grown there. The power radiating from it was palpable, leaving a bittersweet taste on Shya's tongue.

Slowly, it came forward. Shya wasn't sure what she'd expected, but it wasn't this.

When it was close enough, she saw the black-pinned eyes behind the mask. The blown pupils were ringed in red, the shade of which suggested burning to Shya. There was mercy in the gaze, but also madness, and Shya didn't know which would've been better to see. Underneath both was a shard of cold reason, a logic crafted by a different set of values.

Lifting a hand, it held out another mask in front of it, level with Shya's face.

It glistened wetly, putting Shya in mind of semen, and she wasn't surprised it fit well as it was placed over her face. She understood it was something only a parent could've made.

Carefully, Namael picked over the ancient-looking

crown growing from the subject's head. Rather than grafts, he'd used the last of his precious blood, Shya's in fact, to reshape the skull itself.

The procedure was one he'd never attempted before, the reason being the unpredictable nature of such a substance on the human body. Legs and arms were one thing, the head quite another.

The sign refused to form. At times, he saw it clearly, but as soon as it came, it went. He was put in mind of trying to light a candle against a stiff breeze. Only slowly did he understand its fleeting nature was the essence of it. When it appeared, time became fluid; moments passed between his fingers without sensation or awareness. It was as though he woke up after these times, but without falling asleep.

Namael understood the shape he'd worked the skull into, but it was entirely alien to him. He knew it and didn't at the same time.

Whatever agency remained within his subject was not life; it was more and less than the monsters asleep in their cages.

"It is ready."

Namael wondered how long the androgyne had watched him for. Slipping forward from the shadows, it palmed a long-bladed scalpel from a nearby tray and drew its length across its own throat.

Dark blood spilled from the cut, spattering across the body on the wheel. It was smiling as it pitched forward, sprawling across the now-twitching subject.

The King in Yellow broke free of its bonds and sat up. When it turned its hands to test them, the joints popped loud enough to make Namael jump. Namael dragged a boot heel across the floor as he stepped back. The King turned at the sound, and Namael saw the sign forming and reforming above its head.

It resolved for less than the span of one breath, but it was clearer than it had been before. Clearer even than should've been possible.

Time's meaning ceased. It could have lasted a minute, or it could have lasted days. When it began to move again, Namael found his chamber in ruins.

The cages were still closed, but some of the monsters had thrown themselves against the bars, battering their heads and arms against them until pulped to nothing. Those that still moved were of another kind, tumorous amalgams of flesh, muscle, and gristle, mewling from too many wet-lipped mouths.

Something rustled and huffed nearby, behind the curtain to his sleeping area. Namael fled, already knowing what would confront him outside.

Carcosa was as in his dream.

The shadows offered the best protection these days. The daylight, such as it was, brought other things into the streets besides the mobs of masks. Namael grew to distrust the silence, for it was usually when it was most quiet that the first screams would echo from the crumbling stone.

Carcosa was *his* now; there was no right or wrong to it. The King simply was and a force of nature could not be judged.

In the sky above, Namael glimpsed the maelstrom. It

was a circled bruise around an eye of purest black. Already the first of the black stars were winking into life. He could move soon and be about his work.

Namael understood how his subjects must've felt. Retaining enough shreds of reason to know what was missing.

Carcosa was his canvas now and the King had marked his leavings with his sign. He seemed pleased with what Namael was capable of, but he knew he could do so much more.

A boy, scrawny and filthy from head to foot from weeks of living in shit, ran from cover. Namael stayed stock-still in the shadow, his eyes never leaving the child as he ran. It was better if the canvas was as new as possible, all the better to work with. They were more pliable.

Copyright

More from R.L. Robinson at Digital Fiction Publishing Corp.

A Moment of Clarity: Digital Science Fiction Short Story (Cosmic Hooey

First Contact: Digital Science Fiction Anthology (Short Story Collection Book 1)

Across the Terminator: Digital Science Fiction Short Story (Cosmic Hooey)